"WE MADE QUITE A TEAM, LAURIE," CRAIG SAID. "AND I MISSED YOU WHILE YOU WERE GONE."

"Oh, come on, Craig," Laurie blurted. "Don't try and kid me. You were probably so busy chasing good-looking programmers that you didn't give me a thought."

Craig stared at her as though he couldn't believe what she'd just said. "What's wrong?" he asked.

"Nothing's wrong. But don't try to make something more out of the past than was really there. The two of us were just colleagues, and you didn't give me a second thought when I left. Now that I'm back, the only thing that's really changed is the way I look. Is that why you're finally taking me out?"

His green eyes glinted into her dark ones. Irrational though it was, he felt a surge of pleasure in the realization that Laurie DiMaria wasn't going to let him think of her as just another pretty face.

CANDLELIGHT ECSTASY ROMANCES®

MISTAKEN IMAGE

Alexis Hill Jordan

A CANDLELIGHT ECSTASY ROMANCE®

Published by
Dell Publishing Co., Inc.
1 Dag Hammarskjold Plaza
New York, New York 10017

Dell ® TM 681510, Dell Publishing Co., Inc.

Candlelight Ecstasy Romance®, 1,203,540, is a registered
trademark of Dell Publishing Co., Inc., New York, New York.

ISBN: 0-440-15698-X

Printed in the United States of America
First printing—March 1985

To Our Readers:

We have been delighted with your enthusiastic response to Candlelight Ecstasy Romances®, and we thank you for the interest you have shown in this exciting series.

In the upcoming months we will continue to present the distinctive sensuous love stories you have come to expect only from Ecstasy. We look forward to bringing you many more books from your favorite authors and also the very finest work from new authors of contemporary romantic fiction.

As always, we are striving to present the unique, absorbing love stories that you enjoy most—books that are more than ordinary romance. Your suggestions and comments are always welcome. Please write to us at the address below.

Sincerely,

The Editors
Candlelight Romances
1 Dag Hammarskjold Plaza
New York, New York 10017

CHAPTER ONE

The cherry blossoms in Ann Arbor were every bit as lovely as the ones she'd left behind in Japan, Laurie DiMaria thought, looking appreciatively at the pink and white flowering trees that screened the Russel Corporation's parking lot. They softened the lines of the glass and concrete building toward which she was headed. And as she took in the beauty of their spring promise, her step was buoyant.

The trees had also been in bloom when she'd left for her year abroad. Only then their fragile beauty had seemed to mock her. But now, in so many ways, she was coming back to Ann Arbor a new person.

The thought made her take a quick glance at her petite, dark-haired reflection in the smoked glass door. Reassured by what she saw, Laurie stepped inside the foyer and stopped at the guard station.

"Who are you here to see?" the familiar-looking gray-haired man at the desk inquired.

Laurie giggled at the uniformed guard. "Don't you recognize me, Bob?" she asked, proffering her old security pass.

The stocky man, who had greeted her almost every morning for the three years before she'd left on her temporary assignment, stared at her face and then down at the photograph on the plastic rectangle. The expression of puzzlement on his lined face made Laurie's grin widen.

"Is it really you, Miss DiMaria?" he asked, his eyes widening.

"It's really me," she assured him. And then, she added, "Only minus forty-five pounds."

He goggled at her. "You look like a movie star. I really *wouldn't* have recognized you. What happened? Didn't you like Japanese food?"

Laurie smiled again. "Not at first. But now I'm one of its biggest fans," she said with a wink as she retrieved her identification and made her way past him to the bank of elevators lining one wall.

"You'd better get another picture taken," he called after her. "If the new man is on duty, he'll never let you in with the old one. You look so different you might as well be in disguise."

As she waited for the doors to slide open, Laurie mulled over Bob's words. *A disguise,* she mused. He was more right than he knew, for sometimes now she really did feel as though she were walking around in disguise. Mostly it was fun, but sometimes it was disturbing. She glanced down at the image on her pass. She hadn't really looked at it when she took it out of the drawer this morning. But she could see Bob's point. The plump face of the woman in the photograph bore very little resemblance to the delicate, high-boned countenance that she had confronted in the smoked glass moments before.

The elevator doors slid open, and she stepped inside, her heart beating a bit more rapidly under the tailored jacket of her azalea pink linen suit. For this first day back on the job, she had chosen the outfit carefully. The rich color looked good against her flawless olive skin and emphasized the velvety black of her smooth, thick hair. Though her hair reached well below her neckline, she now had it tucked neatly into a sophisticated twist.

Laurie swallowed as the elevator slid to a stop at the second floor. At any moment she was likely to run into some of the people she had worked with a year ago. And they, too, were bound to react to the dramatic change in her appearance. How would she handle that?

The question was answered almost instantly when the chrome doors opened and two men got on. The taller of the two she knew very well. For a wild moment her heart seemed to stop beating as her gaze skated over his lean, fit body in its elegantly tailored dark blue business suit. Unlike her, he hadn't changed a whit. His thick reddish brown hair was still brushed back stylishly. Under dark brows, his green eyes were still intelligently humorous. But that humor was leavened by the uncompromising thrust of his cleft chin below his expressive lips. When those green eyes glanced her way, she hastily averted her gaze and pretended to be fascinated by the lighted numerals that announced the elevator's ascent.

Yet her mind was racing like a windup toy. Had Craig Lawson recognized her? she wondered. So far he'd shown no sign, though she could sense his speculative glance on her profile. He was busy talking about a software design problem with his companion, and as she listened to the mellifluous tone of his deep voice a little shiver ran up her spine. In fact, in these close quarters her whole body was reacting to his presence, reacting in a way she found highly disillusioning.

She almost sighed at the realization. Although he certainly couldn't know it, Craig Lawson had been a big factor in her decision to accept an overseas assignment. She'd wanted to get away from him, needed to escape from the gnawing unhappiness of being helplessly drawn to a man who couldn't see her as anything but a plump and jolly colleague. She'd thought during the past year that she had cured herself of her hopeless obsession with him. But maybe nothing had actually changed after all.

The thought made her unconsciously purse her lips. No, that wasn't true. It was simply the surprise of bumping into him so suddenly that had knocked her off-balance. She could handle her reaction to Craig now. He'd never again get under her skin the way he had in the old days.

It was then that she realized how absurdly she was behaving. Seconds earlier she'd been wondering how she would handle herself with her colleagues. And here she was setting herself up to look like a fool when the man at her side finally did figure out her identity. She should have said hello the minute he entered the elevator.

It was too late now. The car had stopped at her floor. Maybe she'd just been imagining his interest and he really hadn't been paying her any special attention. The next time she encountered him, she'd have a chance to redeem herself.

She was not to have that option, however. For when she stepped out into the tiled corridor, Craig followed.

"I know this is going to sound like a line," he admitted as he came up next to her, "but you look awfully familiar. Haven't I seen you around here before?"

Laurie stopped and turned in his direction. This was the moment for honesty, yet something in his expression changed her mind. His green eyes were surveying her with warm male interest, and an appreciative smile was curving his mouth. Craig Lawson had certainly never looked at Laurie DiMaria that way before. In fact, in the past, when he'd

10

sought her out, it had sometimes been to ask her advice about other women.

"I used to work here. But I haven't been around lately," she said, an impish spark of humor beginning to light the depths of her dark eyes as she hedged the question. In a quite uncharacteristic gesture she found herself lowering her long dark lashes so that she could gaze up at him flirtatiously through their thick screen. Apparently, she thought whimsically, the new Laurie knew some tricks that the old one hadn't even dreamed of.

Craig responded to her feminine ploy with the enthusiasm of King Kong at the first sight of Fay Wray. Taking an assertive step toward her, he deepened his smile. At the same time his eyes crinkled at the corners as he turned on the considerable charm that had swept so many women off their feet.

"Well, I can't imagine how I didn't get to know you before. What department did you work in?"

Laurie had to look down at her toes to keep him from seeing the grin that was tugging at the corners of her lips.

"You know, I don't understand why I can't place you," he went on. "Your voice is so familiar. Were you on the switchboard?"

At that Laurie couldn't repress a giggle. "No, I wasn't. I'm sorry, but I'm already late for an appointment." Pointedly she looked at her watch.

The handsome man who had followed her out of the elevator looked genuinely regretful. "In that case why don't we try and get together later? I'm Craig Lawson; what's your name?"

The introduction made it impossible for Laurie to keep a straight face. Breaking into laughter, she briefly laid her hand on his arm. "Craig, honestly, don't you recognize me?"

Obviously confused, he only stared at her.

"I'm Laurie—Laurie DiMaria," she informed him.

As Craig's jaw dropped, she took the opportunity to make her getaway. Turning, she disappeared quickly into the door on her left. It opened onto the office of corporate vice-president Martin Penwaithe, with whom she was to meet before she briefed his staff after lunch.

Dumfounded, Craig gaped as her tidy little bottom swayed out of sight behind Penwaithe's door. *Laurie DiMaria,* he thought, staggered by the revelation. But how could that be? The Laurie DiMaria he'd known had been a short, plump girl whose round features had disappeared behind a mop of frizzy hair. She'd been a smart woman with a great sense of humor, and he'd always had a lot of respect for her. In fact, they'd been friends. He'd certainly never have dreamed of flirting with her.

For a moment he stood staring at Penwaithe's closed door, visualizing the brunette beauty who'd just had some fun at his expense. Now he understood why she'd looked hauntingly familiar. The weight loss and the new hairstyle had thrown him. That wasn't surprising. But he should have recognized those big dark eyes that he'd always admired.

As he finally turned away to head down the hall, Craig wondered if Laurie was the reason Penwaithe had called a meeting of the team developing the Archimedes educational package.

Craig had intended to spend the next hour preparing for that meeting. Instead, when he sat down behind his desk, he found himself tipping his chair back and continuing to think about the woman who'd captured his attention in the eleva-

12

tor. Before she'd left Ann Arbor, they'd had some pretty soul-searching discussions. In fact, he remembered now with a faint feeling of discomfort around his collar, he'd told her things about himself that he'd never revealed to other women. With that kind of relationship why hadn't he seen her inherent beauty? Did that mean he'd never really looked at her? If so, why not?

The question was disturbing, and he was still pondering it when he strolled into the executive conference room that afternoon. Though he made a point of looking casual, he had actually forced himself not to arrive ten minutes early. Still, he couldn't keep from looking eagerly at the door every time someone came through it.

When Laurie finally arrived, he could see he wasn't the only man who'd been taken by her new loveliness. She was chatting with a very attentive Walt Sheridan, who was looking at her like a dessert addict contemplating a strawberry sundae. Craig frowned, wondering with a little twinge of jealousy if she'd already agreed to a date with the project's senior programmer. On the spot Craig decided to assign the fellow to a task that would keep him out of Laurie's bailiwick.

Though she'd looked like a delicious bit of femininity when she'd come into the room, the moment the meeting started she was all business.

There were some preliminary reports, and then Mr. Penwaithe introduced her. "Our next presentation will be from Laurie DiMaria, who's just back from a year at Hyohoto," he began, unconsciously smoothing the few strands of hair that did nothing to diffuse the reflection of the overhead fluorescents on his bald pate.

After her boss's glowing introduction Laurie took a moment to look out over the group of engineers and computer scientists. She couldn't help smiling at the astonished expressions on many of their faces. Until she'd left, she'd worked closely with most of these people. But she knew that, like Craig, they remembered Laurie DiMaria as an overweight frump, not as the svelte, fashionably dressed woman she had become. Laurie was not vain, yet she enjoyed a pleasurable moment of personal triumph.

But once she got into her presentation, she pushed all such thoughts to the back of her mind and became totally absorbed in her complicated subject.

"As you know, Hyohoto was the low bidder on the Archimedes hardware," she said, referring to the comprehensive educational package Russel was about to market. "I know some of you had reservations about giving the contract to a foreign company." For an instant her gaze met Craig's. He was in charge of the software for Archimedes, and he'd been one of those who'd objected to the foreign alliance. Quickly she looked away. "But," she resumed, "I want to assure you they've done a fantastic job. Because of their efforts, I believe we're going to be able to offer a very competitive product."

She paused again to look around the room. All eyes were on her. The Russel Corporation had a lot of money riding on this collaboration. And if something went wrong, it was quite possible that the company would have to do some belt tightening, including reducing the number of technical personnel. Since these people's jobs might be at stake, she held their full attention.

A few years ago, when Archimedes was still in the design stages, it had seemed like a shoo-in. But the recent number of disasters in the computer industry was becoming a sick joke. Even established firms, which had seemed to have their markets sewn up, had lost millions of dollars over the past

14

few years. Some had even declared bankruptcy. And layoffs in California's Silicon Valley were legion.

Laurie knew some of these thoughts must be in everyone's mind as she went on to detail the technical specifications of the Hyohoto equipment and then began to answer questions.

Although she fielded the queries adroitly, it was impossible for Laurie not to be aware of Craig's scrutiny. He was leaning forward attentively near the other end of the long conference table. Though she tried to tell herself that he was just very interested in the content of her report, she couldn't shake the feeling that his rapt attention was actually personal. If she hadn't known better, she might have thought the man was mentally undressing her.

In fact, he was. As she paced up and down in her demure business suit, Craig's imagination was slowly removing her jacket and then untying that sweet little bow at her neck. The buttons came next, and then he was slipping the garment from her shoulders and picturing the lacy bra beneath. Her skin and hair were dark; did that mean her nipples would be dusky? From what he could see, her breasts were small and high. He was having no trouble imagining his hands caressing them into a response.

Leaning back in his chair, he shifted to ease the discomfort he was suddenly feeling in the lower portions of his body. What was wrong with him? he wondered. He didn't usually drift off into erotic fantasies in the middle of a business meeting, but since he had encountered Laurie that morning, his mind had taken a lot of uncharacteristic turns.

As she picked up the pointer to indicate a pie-shaped wedge on her graph, Laurie was conscious of a heated sensation in her breasts which she somehow knew was connected to Craig's intense scrutiny. It was only by an effort of will

15

that she was able to appear cool and poised during that part of her presentation.

She didn't have much experience with the sensual electricity that often hovered in the atmosphere between men and women who were attracted to each other. But Craig was treating her to several hundred kilowatts as she stood fending off questions from his subordinates. And she would have had to be a grounded wooden post not to have responded.

Although no one would have guessed, by the time the session finally broke up she was definitely feeling jolted. Craig's gaze had been pinned to her for the past forty-five minutes, and as people began to drift away from the conference room, she instinctively knew that he was going to try to take up the conversation that she had broken off in the hall that morning. When he pushed back his chair, she found herself turning again toward Walt Sheridan, who was now hovering at her side.

"Well, what do you think about Hyohoto's new chips?" she asked brightly, allowing him to take her arm and guide her toward the door.

Out of the corner of her eye she could see Craig watching them with narrowed eyes. The effect was to make her even more animated as she smiled vibrantly up at the surprised and pleased-looking programmer.

However, the expression on Laurie's face as she drove back to her new apartment later that afternoon was a lot more subdued. She'd expected her old colleagues to treat her differently because of her changed appearance. But she certainly hadn't been prepared for the enthusiastic response she'd received from the male contingent.

The youngest daughter in a family that "lived to eat," she'd grown up overweight and had never been Miss Popularity. In college her one tentative venture into romance had ended badly when she discovered that the guy she was dating was really just interested in her ability to get him through calculus. After she had broken off the relationship, she consoled herself with food and became even heavier than before.

When she was graduated and started work with the Russel Corporation, things looked brighter. The engineering job suited her talents, and she rose quickly through the ranks. For a time she was able to convince herself that she was cut out to be a career woman and that her lack of dates didn't matter. But when Craig Lawson joined the company, all that changed. They developed a close working relationship —and what she thought of as a strong friendship—very quickly. Almost as quickly Laurie began to realize that it was much more than that for her. Yet Craig was an extremely attractive and charming man who could have any woman he wanted.

Knowing she could never compete with the beauties he invariably dated, Laurie had grabbed at the opportunity to spend a year in Japan as though she were being offered a lifeline. In that new environment she had been convinced that she'd freed herself from the undertow of Craig's sexual magnetism. But five minutes with the man had apparently put her right back in the sea of swirling emotions she'd thought she'd escaped. How would she keep her head above water now?

Blinking, Laurie realized that she'd pulled into the blacktop parking lot of the new high-rise where she'd just taken an apartment. Its particular appeal for Laurie was its location—only a few blocks from the neighborhood where her sister, Sandy Campana, lived with her professor husband and their two elementary schoolers. Three years apart, the sisters had always been close, and it had been Sandy and her family whom Laurie had missed the most while she'd been away.

I wonder if she'll mind if I stop by a little later to pick up some of the stuff I stored in her garage, Laurie thought as she changed into jeans and a T-shirt and then dialed her sister's number.

"Sure. Come on over," Sandy said enthusiastically. "I've been dying to sit down and gossip."

Ten minutes later Laurie was pulling up in front of Sandy's rambling two-story Victorian house. With its rounded front turret and soft gray paint, the house looked like something out of a gothic novel. But the collection of children's toys on the wide front porch and the brightly painted flower boxes at the upper windows changed the image considerably.

As soon as Laurie nosed her car into the narrow, overgrown cement drive, the back door flew open, and Sandy stepped out, a broad smile lighting her rounded face. Pleasantly plump, she was a slightly older version of what Laurie had been, except that Sandy had always been too contented with her life to use food as a panacea. What's more, she was married to a man who adored her well-rounded body.

"Come on in and sample my new lasagna recipe," Sandy said as Laurie followed her back up the stairs and into the kitchen. "I'm trying out some whole wheat pasta."

Laurie shook her head and started to chuckle. "Stop tempting me. I'm not eating that kind of stuff between meals anymore."

Sandy slapped her forehead with her hand. "Sorry. It's taking me a bit of time to get used to my sister the Jaclyn Smith clone," she said good-naturedly. "But I've got some carrot sticks in the refrigerator for the kids. Want some of those?"

"Listen, get over the idea that you've got to feed me whenever I come over," Laurie said insistently. "A cup of tea will do just fine."

Her older sister nodded. "Okay. But you do eat dinner, don't you?"

"Don't be silly. Of course I do."

"Then have it with us. You can fill up on salad if you don't want a lot of lasagna."

"It's a deal," Laurie said, following her sister into the kitchen. Like the rest of the house, it was old-fashioned and high-ceilinged. Even with Sandy's extra income as a counselor at the University Health Service, the couple had not been able to afford to renovate it. The sink was still the chipped porcelain original, but the chief cook had insisted on a new stove and refrigerator. As she began layering the lasagna she was to serve for dinner that evening, she turned and gave her younger sister an appraising look.

"I still can't get over the change in you. Is that really my little sister sitting over there looking as if she had stepped out of a fashion magazine? You know, it really wasn't very nice not to warn me. When you got off the plane last week, I nearly fainted. And now that we've got some time to talk, I think you should tell me your secret. How did you do it?"

Laurie made a little face. Starting with her mother, she'd already had to tell several people this story. Doubtless she'd be reciting it many more times before the month was out. "No secret, really," she began. "When I first got to Japan, I was so homesick I hardly wanted to eat. And," she added wryly, "the truth is I wasn't tempted by the food. After a life devoted to pasta and mozzarella, seaweed, cold rice, and desiccated octopus didn't really turn me on."

Sandy looked horrified. "Don't tell me that's all they eat over there?"

"No, but it took me awhile to discover how good Japanese cuisine really is. Anyway, by that time I'd already lost twenty pounds. One day I took a good look at myself in the mirror and realized that even though my clothes were hanging on me, I liked what I saw."

Sandy nodded. "I'll bet."

"Well, then I really started taking the whole thing seriously."

"What do you mean?" her sister asked, sprinkling the last of the Parmesan on top of the lasagna and sticking the pan in the refrigerator.

Laurie was so wrapped up in her story now that her eyes had a faraway look. "I mean I got some books on nutrition and found out what it was going to take to lose some more weight and keep it off. Then I joined a gym. The Japanese are even more body-conscious than we are, and there are lots of health clubs around."

Fascinated, Sandy sat down opposite her sister at the table. "But your hair and face look different, too—and your clothes are stunning."

Looking down at her sweat shirt and jeans, Laurie grimaced.

"Oh, you know what I mean," Sandy said. "Those aren't the real you anymore."

"Sometimes I wonder who is the real me," Laurie admitted quietly. "You know I never used to pay much attention to how I looked. I guess it's because I didn't think enough of myself to care," she added reflectively. "But once I got started on this self-improvement kick, I figured I might as well go all the way. So I splurged on a consultation at one of Tokyo's fanciest salons. They cut the last of that awful perm out of my hair and showed me some makeup tricks." Laurie began to giggle. "Honestly, when I left the place, I wouldn't have recognized myself."

Sandy studied her sister with a speculative expression. "So what's the net result?" she finally asked. "You certainly look like a different person now. But do you feel different inside?"

Laurie opened her mouth and then closed it as she searched her mind for an accurate reply. "Up until today I thought I was different," she confessed. "But now I'm not so sure."

CHAPTER TWO

"Listen, I'm tired of talking about myself," Laurie protested. "But if it's okay with you, I'd like to pick up some of those boxes I left in your garage."

"Sure," Sandy said. "But it's going to take a van, and a shotgun," she added with a grin, "to get that great furniture of yours out of our living room."

"Forget the shotgun. I was going to offer you that furniture anyway," Laurie told her, pushing her chair back from the table and standing up. "A year in the Orient has changed my taste. I'm having some black lacquered cabinets and tables and a really magnificent screen that I splurged on shipped back here, and they wouldn't go with overstuffed chintz."

Sandy's eyes widened. "Laurie, that's really good furniture. Are you sure you want to give it up?"

"Absolutely."

"At least let me pay you."

Laurie shook her head, knowing her sister's budget all too well. "You can pay me back by helping me with the stuff in the garage. Your station wagon will haul a whole lot more than my little Datsun."

"Sure," Sandy said. "But what are you going to sit on in the meantime?"

"I guess I'm going to have to get a couch and a table and chairs this weekend."

"Don't you need a bed, too?" Sandy asked, following her out the door to the backyard.

"You're not going to believe this, but I got used to sleeping on those Japanese mats—you know, futons. I'm not even sure I'm going to get a bed."

Sandy shook her head. "Were you actually in Japan or did you spend the last year on an alien spaceship?" she asked. "Are you really my sister? The Laurie I knew went in for supersoft mattresses and four-poster beds."

"I'm truly your sister," the petite brunette assured her with a smile before turning to the stack of cartons she'd left behind a year ago.

Half an hour later they had managed to get everything to the parking lot of Laurie's apartment building.

"Listen," she suggested, "let's pile all the boxes by the door. That way we can fill the elevator and just make one or two trips upstairs."

Wiping a rather grimy hand across her brow, Sandy agreed. Soon there was a mountain of cartons by the apartment's service entrance. But while Laurie still looked fresh and energetic, her sister was looking considerably the worse for wear. She was just struggling with one of the smaller boxes when she happened to glance over Laurie's shoulder. "Is that the manager over there looking at us as if we needed to be redirected to the city dump?" she whispered.

Cautiously Laurie turned and peered in the direction her sister had indicated. Watching them with open interest was a tall, good-looking blond in a jogging suit.

Catching Laurie's eye, he flashed a wide grin. "You two look as if you could use some help." As he spoke, he began to stroll toward them.

23

Automatically Laurie opened her mouth to refuse the offer. But Sandy cut her off. "We sure could," she called enthusiastically.

Laurie, who'd already had enough of fending off overly friendly men at work, glared at her sister. But Sandy cheerfully ignored the expression. "We could really use some help with this one," she said, pointing to a large crate of dishes that both of them together had found difficult to maneuver from the car.

The newcomer, however, had no trouble with it at all. Having hoisted it to his shoulder, he began to reach for another box as well.

"My name is Art Frazier, by the way. You must just be moving in. Are you roommates?" he asked, giving Laurie a smile that would have melted the iceberg that sank the *Titanic.*

"We're sisters," Sandy piped up and then went on to tell him their names. "I live with my husband and family a few blocks away. Laurie is the single girl with the new apartment."

His smile, if possible, brightened. But Laurie was too busy aiming a murderous look at the blabbermouth beside her to notice.

After Art had cheerfully brought up the last of the boxes and Laurie had finally managed to close her apartment door, she turned to her sister with a scowl. "What were you trying to do, set me up with that jock?"

"What's the harm in getting to know your neighbors?" Sandy answered the question with one of her own. "Anyway, I thought he was cute."

After pulling out one of the metal folding chairs at the card table she'd lent her sister, Sandy sat down with a sigh.

"But if you don't want to talk about him, here's another subject I can suggest. You know how bureaucracies often assign the least appropriate person to do a job? Well, guess what kind of support group I'm supposed to be leading next week at the counseling center?"

Laurie lifted an eyebrow. "What?"

"Weight reduction." Sandy snorted. "Can't you just see it: the girl who never met a carbohydrate she didn't like telling overweight college students how to stay thin? I guess the center thinks that if you have a degree in counseling, you can pull off anything. But in this case I'm really going to need some help." She paused and beamed at her sister. "And I think I've figured out who's going to give it to me," she announced, eyeing Laurie's svelte form.

Laurie almost dropped the stack of dishes she was carrying to the dishwasher. "Me? I've never counseled anybody in my life," she protested.

"But think of what a role model you are," Sandy said persuasively and then proceeded to demolish all of Laurie's objections. "I don't need you every week," she said in conclusion. "Just the first session and then maybe a follow-up at the end of the semester."

Thoughtfully Laurie began to unwrap some more dishes. "It's not as though my social life were going to keep me so busy that I wouldn't have the time to help you out," she admitted.

Sandy stared at her. "Laurie," she said hesitantly, "you may not have dated a lot in the past. But you must know that's not how it's going to be from here on out. Look at the way Art fell all over himself to help you. And I'll bet the men at your office aren't any different."

"Yeah." Laurie agreed cynically. "They're friendly all

right. The trouble is, I don't know how to handle all the attention."

Sandy waited for her to continue.

"Most of them knew me before and didn't show a bit of interest. So why are they coming on to me now? It's only because I look different. And it's not just that. I'm twenty-seven years old, and I've never had anything you could really call a relationship with a man. I'm not sure I can handle it now—at least not right away. To be honest with you, I feel as if I'm walking around in someone else's body. I need time to get adjusted to the new Laurie myself."

Sandy got up and put her arm around her sister's slender shoulder. "Gee, kid, and here I was thinking that you had it all now. But you're right. You need to gain as much self-confidence dealing with the male half of the human species as you do in dealing with those computers over at the Russel Corporation."

Sandy nibbled on her knuckle while she studied her sister. "On the other hand," she continued, beginning to sound like the counselor that she was, "you shouldn't sit home, afraid to take the plunge. Isn't there somebody you liked before that you could establish a different relationship with now?"

When Laurie didn't answer, Sandy snapped her fingers. "Wasn't there a guy named Craig Lawson you used to talk about a lot? I got the feeling that you were pretty good friends with him. Is he still around?"

Laurie's expression was guarded. Trust her sister to zero in on just what she didn't want to discuss. "Yes, Craig's still around."

"Well then," Sandy continued enthusiastically, "maybe he's just the person to start with."

It was hard for Laurie to repress an almost hysterical giggle. "Sis," she said, beginning to polish the already spot-

26

less stove, "I know you mean well, but you really don't know anything about how things are between me and Craig." She took a deep breath and then turned to face her sister again. "I would never have admitted this to you before, but actually I was crazy about him. I spent that year in Japan getting over him. I certainly don't want to get hung up on the man again."

Sandy looked astonished. "So that's why you used to talk about him so much. I guess I should have realized." Then a speculative gleam lit up her eyes. "Say, did he have anything to do with this transformation?"

Laurie flushed. "Maybe. I'm not even sure myself," she answered. "All I know is that I don't want to get caught in a one-way relationship with him the way I was before."

"But, Laurie, things are different now," her sister protested. "You can't know what your relationship will be with him now unless you give it a chance. Besides, the new Laurie might go out with him and find out she isn't interested anymore."

Laurie wondered later if some telepathic waves from this conversation had reached Craig. Or maybe he had simply been trying to call her while she was out and had finally gotten through. At any rate, only a few minutes later the phone rang. When she picked up the receiver, he was at the other end of the line.

"Craig." She couldn't keep from squeaking his name in surprise when she heard his deep voice. At the same time her gaze flew guiltily to Sandy's face.

But her sister's reaction to the phone call was quite different from hers. She gave Laurie a big grin and made no bones about being very interested in what she could hear of the conversation. At first it was obvious that the two speakers were merely exchanging pleasantries about the weather and

27

the Russel Corporation. But Craig soon got to the real point of his call.

"Laurie," he said, "you and I have a lot of catching up to do. How about dinner tonight?"

"Sorry, I already have an invitation for tonight."

"Oh?"

"I'm having dinner at my sister's place," she quickly added. Looking across the room, she saw Sandy roll her eyes toward the ceiling before getting up from her chair. After crossing to Laurie's side, she began to mouth words that her sister couldn't understand but that she suspected were a hasty withdrawal of her dinner invitation if something better had materialized. Shaking her head and waving her hand, Laurie tried to concentrate on what Craig was asking.

"Then how about this Friday or Saturday? Are you booked up that far in advance?" he asked, making it clear that he wasn't going to be put off easily.

"Friday or Saturday," she murmured, trying to take in the meaning of his words. It was a bit hard to concentrate because she was watching Sandy madly scribbling a note on a paper napkin. When it was thrust under her nose, the message read, "Go out with him, you fool!"

Despite the interference in her affairs, Laurie couldn't help grinning.

"Listen, you sound kind of distracted," Craig was saying. "Did I call at a bad time?"

"Well, I was trying to get some stuff unpacked," Laurie said, stalling as she watched Sandy hurriedly start to compose what was undoubtedly another command. Somehow she felt as though she were the straight man caught in the middle of a comedy routine; only no one had given her a script.

28

"All you have to do is tell me which is better for you, Friday or Saturday, and I'll let you get back to your chores."

"SAY YES," Sandy's next napkin insisted in large capital letters.

Apparently the only way to get Sandy off her back was to acquiesce. "Yes," Laurie almost shouted.

"Great. Does that mean you're free both Friday and Saturday?" Craig asked.

Laurie shot her sister a murderous look. "Um, uh," she said flounderingly and then finally blurted out, "Friday. Friday will be fine."

"Good, I'll pick you up at seven," Craig said. "But it really does sound as though I were keeping you from some serious unpacking. So I'll let you go."

When she hung up the receiver, Laurie glared at her sister, who only smiled impishly back at her.

"Well, under stress you did the right thing." The counselor congratulated her. "And I really do think you're doing yourself a favor straightening out your relationship with Craig right away instead of stewing about it," she added forcefully.

Was she really doing the right thing? Laurie wondered as she inspected her image in the mirror one last time. She was wearing one of the silk sheaths she'd brought back with her from Japan. A vibrant peacock blue, it molded her slim body perfectly. Though the mandarin collar and cap sleeves were quite demure, the costume managed to be sensual in a way that more blatantly suggestive Western dresses could never achieve. It had the kind of line that would have looked ridiculous on anyone who wasn't pencil slim. It was probably for that reason that Laurie had been unable to

29

resist the purchase. But she hadn't pictured herself wearing it in front of anybody she knew. Now she wondered if she really wanted to look this sexy for Craig. However, it was too late; she didn't have time to change.

As she searched for a distraction, her gaze shifted to her face. She'd spent a lot of time on her hair and makeup. Once again her sable tresses were caught behind her head in a sophisticated French twist. Her only jewelry was the pair of delicately wrought silver pendants that swung from her tiny earlobes. Thoughtfully she touched them with a fingertip the nail of which had been carefully shaped and polished to a deep pink. The woman in the mirror looked assured and poised. How could the image be so different from the reality? Laurie wondered, taking stock of the butterflies dancing wildly in her stomach.

After turning away from the mirror, she walked slowly out into the living room and sat down on the new parson style couch that she'd rushed out and bought the day after Craig's call. The couch, a small Oriental rug, and a new breakfast set in the kitchen were still the only furnishings in the apartment. But at least the place wouldn't look entirely bare when he arrived.

Just then the doorbell rang, and Laurie jumped. Glancing at her watch, she noted that it was five to seven. Craig was early. But obviously she was going to appear just as anxious. Suddenly she felt gauche about being completely ready. Pausing, she slipped off her pearl gray sandals and transferred them to one hand while she opened the door with the other.

"Oh hi, Craig. Sorry, I'm not quite ready," she said apologetically, gesturing toward the shoes.

Craig looked thoughtful. "Gee, I thought I heard the

click of high-heeled shoes hitting the floor. It must have just been my overactive imagination."

Willing herself not to blush, Laurie stepped aside and motioned her date into the living room. Wearing a navy blazer and tan slacks, he was casually handsome. He had the crisp look of a man who had just showered and shaved. As he passed by her, she caught an enticing whiff of lime aftershave. Though she'd seen him every day at work this week, somehow he looked subtly different. Could it have had anything to do with what he was anticipating for the evening? she wondered, walking toward the center of the room and turning to face him.

"Would you like to have a drink while I finish getting ready?" she asked.

He glanced around at the all but empty room. "Where do you hide your liquor?"

Luckily Laurie had purchased a few bar supplies that afternoon. "It's in a kitchen cabinet for the moment," she replied, acknowledging the empty state of the apartment with a grin. "But the selection's rather limited. I can offer you a gin and tonic or a gin and tonic."

"In that case, I accept. But why don't you go ahead and finish getting ready? Just direct me to the makings, and I'll fix us each one."

Though Laurie didn't really like cocktails and had bought the liquor only for guests, she would have felt like a fool explaining that to Craig. Instead, she simply nodded and escaped back into her bedroom to gather her wits about her.

God, what a beginning for a date. She scolded herself as she looked at her watch and then sat down on the bed. She'd have to stay in here for five minutes, she told herself, checking the time again before slowly leaning down and putting her sandals back on. Although she hated to admit it, this

31

was the kind of cat-and-mouse game she'd been playing with Craig all week. While it was still possible, she'd been deliberately avoiding him at work. But the breather she'd given herself was going to come to an abrupt end when the Hyohoto hardware arrived. Before she left for Japan, her position in the company had been very junior to Craig's. Now, though she was still technically a level below him in the scheme of things, her specialized experience on the Hyohoto project meant that she'd be working closely with him on an equal footing. The whole situation made her nervous, and not just because of her complicated feelings for Craig. Nobody had actually tested the Hyohoto equipment with the new version of the software Craig's group had provided. What if something went wrong? It might mean that her professional credibility would be at stake.

Pushing these worrisome thoughts aside, she stood up and surveyed herself in the mirror one last time. *Back to the front lines,* she told herself with a grin. It was ridiculous to think of a simple date as a trial of courage, but somehow she couldn't get out of her head the idea that she was going into battle. When she returned to the living room, Craig was lounging on the couch, looking much too relaxed for combat.

"Your drink's on the pass-through. I would have brought it in, but there was no place to put it," he informed her, watching with open admiration as she crossed in front of him to get it.

Feeling once more self-conscious about the clinging lines of her silk dress, Laurie quickly hoisted the tall cool glass and turned toward Craig. She would have liked to have remained standing where she was. But it was time to sit down. And if she stayed here much longer, it would have been an admission that she was nervous about being close to him. Yet the only place to sit was the couch. Mentally she cursed herself for not buying a chair to go with it. But at the time she'd been thinking in terms of furniture payments, not of logistics, she reminded herself, unconsciously using another military term.

As though reading her mind, Craig smiled innocently and patted the cushion next to him. "Come on and sit down. There are so many demands on your time right now that I never really get a chance to talk to you at work."

So he'd noticed that she'd been making sure to be busy when he was around. Slowly she walked across the room once more, settled herself discreetly at the far end of the couch, and crossed her legs at the ankles—about all the mobility that the tight skirt of the dress allowed. Looking around, she realized that Craig was right. There was no place to put her drink except on the floor. And with her luck tonight, she'd probably kick it over.

Holding up her glass, she shook her head. "Sorry about the lack of furnishings," she said. "But I got rid of my old stuff before I left, and I haven't had much chance to do any shopping."

Taking a swallow of his drink, Craig eyed her trim figure. He couldn't help thinking that she'd certainly gotten rid of an awful lot of excess baggage since she'd left a year ago. All this week he'd been watching her, trying to match the sleek, slightly aloof brunette knockout she'd become with the friendly, bumptious young engineer she'd been. There were points of similarity, of course. She still had the same gorgeous eyes and silvery laugh. And, of course, the sharp mind and quick wit were just as incisive.

Her voice was another matter, however. It had always been slightly husky and low-pitched. But it had never before

33

struck him as sexy, whereas now it made him feel like a cat being stroked with a velvet glove.

There were many other changes as well. The one he had found the most puzzling, however, was her attitude toward him. Before leaving for Japan, she'd been very friendly and open—almost like a puppy anxious for attention. But since she'd come back, for the most part she'd been withdrawn and almost standoffish. Was she worried about the Hyohoto equipment? he wondered. He'd like to think that was all, but he suspected there was something else behind that wary expression in her beautiful dark eyes.

And they were very, very beautiful, he thought, studying her delicately modeled face as she sipped her drink. In that dress, with her hair swept up regally, she looked like an exotic princess. He suddenly sensed how Marco Polo must have felt when new worlds had opened up to him. For Craig, this new Laurie was like an undiscovered jewel somehow transformed by the mysterious Orient. Yet they did have a common background. Maybe he could use some shared memory to reestablish the friendly relationship they'd had before. And maybe if he were lucky, he could use that as a way to bring them even closer together.

The idea made him grin. Just the right sort of incident had popped into his mind.

"What are you thinking about?" Laurie asked.

"About the time Penwaithe had that VIP tour of the research labs scheduled, only to discover at four o'clock in the afternoon the day before that there was a bug in his showpiece software."

Laurie shook her head and smiled. "How could I forget that? You and I had to stay there all night to fix it. And when Penwaithe came through with those bigwigs at nine

34

the next morning, we still weren't quite sure it was going to work."

"But it did, and mostly thanks to you," Craig said complimentarily. "You were a real trouper."

Laurie looked down at her drink, the warm memories suddenly congealing. *A real trouper,* she thought. *Wasn't I just that?* That was certainly the way Craig had always seen her. Spending the night practically rubbing shoulders with him had strung out her emotions so thin that she'd felt like a wrung-out washcloth. But the night's work hadn't had any such effect on him. When he took her out to breakfast, he hadn't spent much time thanking her for her efforts. Instead, he'd somehow ended up complaining to her about his ex-wife as though Laurie were one of the boys.

As she remembered it, he'd been married young to a gorgeous blonde who'd slept late every morning and never fixed him breakfast. In fact, that was the way he'd got off on the subject: remembering all the cardboard-flavored frozen waffles he'd downed during his brief, unsuccessful marriage. "Susie was beautiful to look at," he'd confided. "But she had no interest in being a wife. When she left me, she made sure she got enough of a settlement to launch her modeling career. I see her now off and on—but only on the covers of fashion magazines."

Remembering that bitter admission, Laurie sipped her gin and tonic and looked at Craig speculatively. Undoubtedly that unsuccessful foray into marriage had molded his attitude toward women. Ever since she'd known him, he'd treated the ones he'd dated like chocolate kisses—delicious while they lasted but definitely ephemeral.

"We made quite a team, Laurie," Craig was saying. "And I missed you while you were gone. In fact, I didn't realize how much until I saw you the other morning in the elevator."

"Oh, come on, Craig," Laurie blurted out. "Don't try to kid me. You were probably so busy chasing good-looking programmers that you didn't give me a thought."

Craig stared at her as though he couldn't believe what she'd just said. Obviously his mention of their previous relationship hadn't set her mind working along the same lines as his.

"What's wrong?" he asked.

Laurie swallowed. She hadn't meant to speak so bluntly. But now that the words were out, she might as well make herself clear.

"Nothing's wrong. But don't try to make something more out of the past than was really there. The two of us were just colleagues, and you didn't give me a second thought when I left. Now that I'm back, the only thing that's really changed is the way I look. Is that why you're finally taking me out?"

Craig was taken aback, startled by her frankness. A flush began to creep up his neck as he realized how his words must have sounded. Her assumption was not really true. He *had* missed her and thought of her from time to time. But she was right about her changed appearance making a difference. Not until they'd met in the elevator had he ever thought of her as a desirable woman he'd like in his bed.

The fact that she'd called him on his changed attitude so quickly and refused to accept his version of their former relationship made him wonder what was really on her mind. Most women were glad to go along with that sort of flattery. Perhaps in the years since his painful divorce he had grown too used to easy conquests.

But that was obviously not going to be the case with the woman sitting at the other end of the couch and looking at him with a glint of defiance in her intelligent dark eyes. And suddenly he was glad because he really didn't want to categorize Laurie DiMaria with the other beauties who had flitted briefly through his bachelor life, leaving no real impact.

His green eyes glinted into Laurie's dark ones. Irrational though it was, he felt a surge of pleasure in the realization that Laurie DiMaria wasn't going to let him think of her as just another pretty face. But along with the pleasure he was feeling very distinctly challenged. Laurie DiMaria was a woman worth having, and he meant to have her.

CHAPTER THREE

Determined to get their date back on course, Craig stood up, crossed to the pass-through, and set down his empty glass. "Where would you like to go to dinner?" he asked.

Laurie was eager to change the subject, too. It would be a long evening if their conversation became a fencing match. But Craig's question made her mind go blank.

"You know how Ann Arbor is. The restaurants are always changing. You'll have to tell me what's good."

"Maybe I should revise my question then. What kind of food do you like? As I recall, you used to be fond of pasta." Pausing, he eyed her slim figure. "Is that still the case?"

Laurie smiled. There'd been a time when she could easily put away a large bowl of spaghetti on her own. Doubtless Craig was aware of the fact. Although he'd been too polite to ask, like everyone else, he was probably curious about her weight loss. But she didn't want to get into that now. It was too personal somehow. "I guess I was, wasn't I?" she answered casually. "But I've learned to prefer lighter cuisine."

"In that case," Craig said, "there's a northern Italian restaurant that I've been pleased with in the new mall. Would you like to try that?"

Laurie smiled. Northern Italian cooking with its veal and chicken dishes in light sauces was a far cry from the heavy pasta productions she'd been brought up on. "Sounds marvelous."

A half hour later, as she sipped her white wine and studied the menu at the Cantina d'Italia, she could see that there were a number of tempting dishes that wouldn't ruin her diet. In fact, it was going to be hard to choose.

As they began their first course, Craig looked approvingly down at the tempting mix of crisp greenery and other vegetables on his plate. "One thing I like about this place is its salads. But I suppose, since you grew up on Italian home cooking, this is par for the course."

Laurie giggled. "My mother and my aunts never even bothered with salad. They went straight for tons of pasta topped by cheese and meat sauce."

Craig raised an eyebrow. "Actually that sounds pretty good to me."

"It was good," Laurie said. "That's why my sister and I grew up plump. Until I went away to college, I didn't know there was any other way to eat, and by then it was too late."

"Obviously it wasn't too late," Craig interjected quickly. "You certainly don't seem to be suffering any ill effects now."

He had just given her an opening to talk about her weight loss, but Laurie was still reluctant to take it. It was a very sensitive subject, one that she wasn't yet ready to share with this man in particular. Instead, she concentrated on her salad for a moment before changing the subject.

"What was dinnertime like at your house when you were a kid?" she asked.

"A struggle for survival," he said jokingly, although an edge to the words belied their playfulness. "I was the youngest in a family of eight, and there was never enough of anything to go around." He looked thoughtfully down at his place setting, memories that darkened his expression parading through his mind. "When my mother put the stew and biscuits on the table, it was every kid for himself. You wouldn't believe how many times I got the short end of the spoon. Actually I think I grew up hungry."

"You're kidding," Laurie said. Craig seemed so much like the man who'd always had everything.

But he shook his head. "No, I was a scrawny, hungry kid from the wrong side of town. And though I've since moved to the higher rent district and filled out, in a lot of ways I'm still very hungry."

As they left the restaurant an hour later, Laurie was still pondering that revealing remark. She hadn't known exactly how to pick up on it, so their conversation had become more inconsequential as they'd enjoyed their veal and chicken entrées.

Nevertheless, the brief description of his family life troubled her. She'd been complaining about the way her mother had overfed her, but the older DiMarias had always given their children warmth and support. Had Craig grown up feeling deprived? And what *exactly* had he meant by "hungry"? Did he mean "hungry" in the material sense? He did dress well and drive a prestigious sports car, but that was no different from the majority of bachelors in his income bracket. Could he be referring to success? she wondered. He had always struck her as ambitious—but not viciously so. As far as she knew, his promotions had been earned on the basis of merit. He'd never climbed up the corporate ladder on the broken backs of his colleagues. And he couldn't mean it literally. He had a leanness that would be impossible for an overeater to maintain.

No, as she thought about it, there was only one area where his behavior might strike her as hungry, and that was the endless parade of good-looking women he had dated since arriving at the Russel Corporation.

Laurie shot him a sideways glance as they strolled down the main thoroughfare of the mall. But was that really being fair? she wondered. The truth was, although he had asked her advice about women a couple of times, most of what she knew about his social life was office gossip. And that could be way off the mark.

"There's a movie theater at the end of the mall." Craig interrupted her thoughts. "Want to find out if there's anything playing that you'd like to see?"

Laurie shrugged. "I've been away so long I don't know any more about current films than I do about the new restaurants in Ann Arbor. In a way I feel almost like a time traveler. You wouldn't believe how much things can change in a year."

"Like what?" Craig asked, taking her elbow and guiding her down the brightly lit promenade.

"Well, I haven't had much time to explore around town, but I have noticed lots of new buildings. And then there's this mall," she added, gesturing at the impressive two-story shopping enclosure they were exploring.

She paused for a moment in front of a window filled with home computers. "They didn't have this kind of place in a shopping mall when I left."

Craig laughed down at her. Then, almost as though they were back on the comfortable terrain of their old friendship, he said banteringly, "Maybe you want to take a busman's holiday, but the store next door looks more interesting." His hand on her elbow, he guided her to the next window. It was full of lacy underwear, including teddies and garter belts, modeled by toothy mannequins that all were posed like jungle cats ready to spring.

If it had been a year earlier, Laurie would have been amused, knowing that he definitely wasn't imagining her in any of those revealing garments. Now she wasn't sure of his intentions. And though she tried to match his light mood, the suggestive display in the window embarrassed her.

It was Craig's turn to shoot his companion a covert glance. The faint flush behind her smooth olive cheeks told him that this sort of joking around was making her uncomfortable.

"The movie's right down there," he pointed out. "And there's a line of people going in. So we may have timed this just right."

Relieved by the change of subject Laurie followed him to the theater entrance.

As Craig drew abreast of the advertising poster, he grinned. "It looks as though fate has determined that we're going to have a busman's holiday after all."

The film being shown was called *High Tech Heist*, and the brightly colored poster depicted a well-dressed young man leaning over a computer terminal. From the screen was pouring a veritable cornucopia of money and luxury items. There were several smaller scenes in the background, one of which showed him in bed with a luscious brunette.

"I read a review of this film, and I've been wanting to see it. It's supposed to be really good," Craig declared enthusiastically.

Laurie hesitated. The picture had an R rating. But that could simply mean a few four-letter words.

"You get in line, and I'll buy the tickets," Craig said. He was obviously eager to see the film. And though Laurie still had some doubts about the rating, she would feel like a fool objecting on that score.

As they entered the lobby, Craig looked toward the refreshment stand. "A movie always means popcorn to me. But I'll get it without butter," he added quickly, seeing her raised eyebrows.

The line was long, and by the time Craig had purchased his mammoth box of salty white kernels, there were few double seats left. They were forced to go almost to the front of the theater in order to sit together.

"Sorry," he said apologetically as the previews flashed on.

"No problem. It makes me feel like a kid again to be sitting in the second row from the front," she told him.

Twenty minutes into the movie she decided that her fears had been groundless. It was a fast-paced comedy thriller with a very appealing hero who called himself Jack Lightfingers. But no sooner did she relax and really begin to enjoy the action than a steamy bedroom interlude between Jack and a lithesome blonde got under way. Laurie was left with no doubt about what had caused the rating. And the sensual action made her squirm in various kinds of discomfort. The underwear display window in the mall had sent her imagination spinning along embarrassing lines, but this was far worse.

As the hero caressed the blonde's full breasts and covered her wriggling body with his, Laurie couldn't help picturing herself and Craig doing something similar. The thought made her breasts feel unaccountably heavy, and an undeniable warmth began centering itself below her abdomen.

What's more, that was only the beginning. Other love scenes with different girls followed at regular intervals. And since she and Craig were sitting so close to the screen, it was almost as if they were in bed with the various celluloid lovers.

Laurie would have been even more disturbed to know

that Craig's reaction was similar to hers, although he was amused by it whereas Laurie was embarrassed.

He had spent a lot of time fantasizing about Laurie's body since that morning in the briefing room. Now he had not only the object of fantasies beside him but the added stimulus of technicolor, larger-than-life visual aids right in front of him. And they became even more graphic as the film progressed. When the brunette from the poster appeared in the omnivorously virile Jack's apartment, things heated up beyond the boiling point.

"Dianna," he was saying on the screen between panting breaths, "you're so goddamn lovely, and I want you so much."

You and everyone else in skirts, Laurie thought, sliding down in her seat as Jack removed the lovely and oh, so willing Dianna's dress and began to unhook her bra. When he lifted her ample breasts and rubbed his face against them, Laurie wished she had her own popcorn box so that she could hide behind it.

To make things worse, she was obviously not the only one in the theater affected by the scene. The noise of heavy breathing behind her neck made her swivel her head to see two teenagers locked in an embrace almost as passionate as the one on the screen. As she took in the wandering hands and glued-together mouths of the youngsters, Laurie's eyes widened, and she quickly jerked her gaze away and turned forward. But she felt her neck prickle with awareness.

Craig, on the other hand, seemed oblivious to what was going on behind him. His eyes were riveted to the screen, almost as though Dianna, with her long raven tresses and gorgeous body, were actually Laurie. He watched the screen in eager anticipation as the hero picked up the woman and carried her to the bed. He couldn't help picturing himself

44

doing something similar with the brunette beauty at his side. How he would like to unzip that silk dress and investigate the flesh it sheathed!

Laurie was glad that the theater was dark. Her skin felt hot, and she knew her face must be bright red. She tried to tell herself that what she was watching was a piece of make-believe. Yet the Technicolor scenes were so vivid and real that it was impossible not to react. Though she kept her face forward, she was very conscious of Craig in the next seat. Unless he were deaf and blind, he had to be reacting to this kind of sexual stimulation.

As though her thoughts were tangible and he'd picked them up, he leaned toward her. "Have you lost interest in the popcorn?" he whispered huskily.

The heat in her face increased so that she was even more unwilling than ever to turn in his direction. "Oh, yes, thanks," she muttered, reaching across to where the open tub of popcorn had been resting in his lap. But since he had considerately picked up the container and held it out toward her, what her searching hand found was the hard flesh of his inner thigh.

Realizing instantly how intimately she had just touched him, she yanked back her hand as though it had come in contact with a burning stove. Her out-of-control reaction only made matters worse. Her retreating hand hit the open carton, scattering white kernels all over both their laps and the floor.

Mortified, Laurie stared down at the mess. Now even more than before she felt like sinking down in her seat. "Oh, God, I'm so sorry. I can't believe I just did that."

"That's okay." Craig reassured her quickly and then laughed. "I guess it's lucky we didn't get it with butter after all."

Looking down, he began to brush the fluffy snack off his light-colored pants and then looked at her skirt. "The oil is going to ruin that beautiful dress," he commented, reaching across and beginning to brush her skirt. But his hands flicking across the silky material covering her thigh only made things worse as far as Laurie was concerned. Despite the embarrassing situation, his touch was too much of a reminder of the attraction he held for her and of where the movie had led her overheated thoughts. Standing up to escape his help, she began to swipe frantically at her skirt.

"Hey, sit down; we can't see the screen," the boy in back of her protested.

Since when had that couple been watching the movie? Laurie wondered, sliding back down in her seat and wishing that there were some graceful way to escape.

Craig, who had been all too aware of her distress, leaned over in her direction. "Why don't we just leave? I think we've lost track of the story line anyway."

Laurie accepted gratefully. But as they headed up the aisle, she felt conspicuous. Many curious faces were turned in their direction. So much for the image of the cool computer professional she'd been cultivating all week, she thought wryly. What would Craig say when they emerged into the brightly lit lobby? she wondered.

But he only looked at her and grinned. "This reminds me of the time when I was a teenager and I spilled cola in my lap during a horror movie. Only, unfortunately, I was wearing white jeans. I had to walk half a mile back home with a stain that drew snickers from everyone who saw me."

"That must have been horrible," Laurie said sympathetically, realizing that what had just happened was really nothing in comparison.

"Actually I think that popcorn incident was well timed. I've seen enough computers for the day."

Laurie nodded, glad that he was exhibiting so much magnanimity. She couldn't have blamed him if he'd been irritated. After all, he'd wanted to see *High Tech Heist,* and her stupid accident had made it almost impossible for them to stay in the theater. But as Craig settled himself in his car and headed out of the parking lot, he seemed perfectly cheerful. What's more, he was apparently determined to put her back at her ease.

"I believe it's a good thing you saved me from the rest of that popcorn. I'd already eaten half the tub when it hit the floor, and it's made me thirsty." He slanted an inquiring glance at her. "Want to stop for ice cream sodas?"

"Not for me," Laurie said. "I've given that kind of thing up. But if you want to have one, I'll be glad to keep you company."

As they paused in front of a red light, he looked at her assessingly. "Giving up ice cream sodas sounds like a fate worse than death."

Laurie laughed. "Not at all. In fact, I've found the fruit shakes I make in my own blender are just as good—and a lot cheaper."

"That sounds interesting. Just what goes into these creations?"

Laurie was enthusiastic about her recipe, and her tone was bubbly. "It's mostly fresh fruit, along with this really good no-calorie sweetener I've found, and some yogurt. I think I've got all the ingredients in the refrigerator. Want to try one?"

"Sure," Craig answered instantly.

The eagerness in his voice gave Laurie pause, and she realized that what she'd just done was invite him into her apartment when she'd planned to say good night outside the door.

"Listen, on second thought, maybe I don't really have enough yogurt."

But Craig was unfazed. "That's okay. Now that you've whetted my appetite, I'm determined to try one of these things. We'll stop and pick up some yogurt."

Fifteen minutes later they arrived at Laurie's door, carrying a bag from a nearby convenience store. As she turned the key in her lock, she mentally kicked herself for having maneuvered herself into a corner. But there was no gracious way out of it now.

"Make yourself comfortable," she called over her shoulder as she headed for her small kitchen. But instead of waiting politely out on the couch, Craig tagged along only a few steps behind.

"I wouldn't miss seeing this for the world," he informed her cheerfully. "If these are as good as you say, I'm going to want to know how to make them."

Laurie quickly flipped on the light and then stood between him and the refrigerator so that she could push the full carton of yogurt she knew was on the top shelf out of sight before removing some fruit. "You have to own a blender to make one of these," she pointed out.

Craig was leaning against the counter, surveying her lazily. "Oh, every self-respecting bachelor who wants to impress his dates with homemade piña coladas owns a blender."

"I'm sure," she replied, thinking of all the dates Craig had probably impressed with his skills as a bartender—and doubtless other skills as well.

"Can I do anything to help?" he asked as she turned to remove an ice tray from the freezer compartment.

"There's hardly anything to do," she said. "I just have to peel a banana and an orange. Besides those, I usually use whatever fruit is in season. Strawberries are good now." As she spoke, she began to rinse and hull several of the glistening red berries.

"Let me peel the orange," Craig said. "My mother always used to toss one in my lunch bag, so I'm good at that."

He wasn't exaggerating. It seemed as though his nimble fingers had dispatched the thick-textured skin from the sectioned fruit in no time. But in the process he spattered his hands with the juice. After setting the peeled orange down on the countertop, Craig automatically began to lick the golden sweetness from his thumb and forefinger. Watching the unconscious gesture from under her eyelashes, Laurie couldn't help noting the primitive sensuality. Suddenly her mouth felt dry, and her fingers trembled on the banana she was peeling. Realizing where her wayward thoughts were once more leading, she hastily sliced the fruit and stuffed it into the blender.

"What now?" Craig asked as he watched with an interested smile.

Quickly Laurie measured the yogurt, dumped it into the container, and followed with several packets of artificial sweetener. After securing the blender's top, she turned the machine on high.

"What about the ice?" Craig asked over the roar of the motor. He had moved directly in back of her and was peering down over her shoulder. She could feel his body heat through the thin silk of her dress, and his breath stirred tendrils of hair on her neck. The effect of his nearness made her hold onto the base of the whirring machine as though it were a life ring in deep water.

"I'll put the ice cubes in one at a time now," she managed

49

to articulate. To her own ears, her voice sounded high and breathless. With fingers that still trembled slightly, she picked up a frozen rectangle and dropped it through the hole in the center of the blender top. Immediately the blades protested with a loud grinding sound and the machine began to vibrate on the countertop.

As she added another cube, Craig leaned even closer and circled her waist with his arms. "Let me steady the base for you," he murmured, reaching for the bottom of the blender.

"You don't have to," Laurie quavered, hastily dropping in several more pieces. But then she realized her mistake. Unable to handle that much ice at once, the little machine began to buck. Craig now had an excellent excuse to lean forward over her shoulders to steady the base—and at the same time press his thighs tightly against her bottom. There was really nothing she could do but stand there praying for the ice to finish grinding.

Was it her imagination, or could she feel Craig's cheek brushing softly against the top of her head? Her knees were so weak now that she had to grip the counter to keep from sagging against him. It seemed like an eternity before her practiced ears told her that the concoction was finally ready.

"I think you can let go now," she whispered.

It took several seconds before Craig complied and stepped back. Drawing a deep, steadying breath into her lungs, she reached up and brought down two tumblers. In another moment she had filled them with the frothy pinkish drink and handed one to Craig.

Looking at her over the rim of the glass, he took a sip and then smiled. "Ummm, delicious," he said. "This really was a much better idea than an ice cream soda."

Laurie wasn't sure about that. But she nodded in agreement as she sampled her drink.

"This tastes so rich you'd swear it was fattening," Craig was saying. As if to emphasize the point, his tongue came out and slowly licked a bit of creamy liquid from his upper lip.

Laurie watched mesmerized as his eyes met hers. "You've got a white mustache, too," he informed her gravely. Then he reached out and ran his finger along the top of her lip. Looking down at the sweet white froth he'd removed, he brought it to his own mouth and tasted it with his tongue. "Delicious," he murmured again.

Maybe it was the increased heat of her own body that made Laurie suddenly conscious of the coldness of the glass she clutched in her hands. Without thinking, she set the tumbler down on the counter and was surprised when Craig followed suit. He was standing very close to her now, so close that she could see the golden highlights that gave his green eyes their rich color. As she watched, they seemed to darken with purpose.

Reaching out, he touched her lips again. And now she was aware of the pungent scent of orange on his fingers.

"What are you doing?" she whispered. But she knew very well what he was going to do. She felt the heat of his breath against her mouth and then his lips, firm but at the same time sweetly persuasive.

It was not a hard, demanding kiss but almost an innocently seductive one—an invitation rather than a command. And Laurie could not help accepting that invitation. With a small sigh, she parted her lips, suddenly eager for the taste and touch of Craig Lawson.

In her inexperience she had not known quite what to expect. It was hard to believe that the brush of his tongue across her inner lips and teeth or the sweetly persuasive pressure of his mouth against hers could bring such intense pleasure.

"Craig," she whispered, her arms moving upward instinctively so that she could anchor herself against his shoulders lest she be swept away by the tide of sensations he was creating.

"Mmmm," he responded, his own arms tightening around her waist in order to pull her more firmly against the hardening length of his body. As he turned to trace the delicate pink curves of her ear with his tongue and nip playfully at the lobe, she found herself clinging to him even more tightly, knowing no other way to cope with the storm of hot feelings he was rousing within her. She had told herself that Craig's attraction to her had nothing to do with her real self —that it was only a superficial reaction to her changed appearance. But that didn't seem to matter now.

She drew in her breath as one of his hands began to investigate the column of her spine, while his lips made a tantalizing journey along her jawline before returning hungrily to her mouth once again. Teasingly his tongue darted between her lips several times, always withdrawing as though he were coaxing her exploration of his own mouth.

She had not thought herself capable of such aggressiveness. In her innocent imaginings she had even wondered whether she would really enjoy kissing in such an intimate way. But Craig had made her as eager to learn as much about him as he wanted to learn about her. Tentatively at first, and then with more assurance, she ran her tongue along his lips and teeth, pausing to savor the new sensations the caresses aroused. Then, with only a slight, trembling hesitation, she breached those outer barriers to return the pleasures he had so recently taught her.

Encouraged by this new show of boldness, Craig began to

feather-stroke his fingers along the sides of her ribs and then moved forward to cup his hands under her breasts.

Laurie drew back slightly. "Craig . . ." she began. But the syllable ended on a sigh as his thumbs found her nipples and began to stroke them to aroused hardness through the silky fabric of her dress and bra. For a moment she was captured by the fevered sensations of the unaccustomed caress, feeling the heat from it surge and course downward through her body. Yet she found the very intensity of her reaction as alarming as his next move.

Leaning forward, Craig sought her mouth with his again while his hands found the zipper at the back of her dress and began to tug it open.

It took him a moment to realize that the impassioned woman he had held in his arms had vanished and that Laurie had brought up her hands and pressed her palms firmly against the front of his chest. "Craig, don't," she said protestingly, the strident note in her voice telling him as much as the words themselves.

"What's wrong?" he asked, drawing back so that his questioning eyes could search her face.

"Don't do that," she repeated, stepping backward and reaching to tug the zipper up to her neckline once again. "I think you'd better leave," she added, aware that she must look and sound like a perfect fool now.

"But I thought . . ." Craig began.

"You thought wrong. Now please, just leave." As she spoke, she turned away, unable to let him see the strong emotions fighting for control of her features. If it had been possible for her to leave the kitchen without brushing past him, she would have. Instead, she simply stood there, holding onto the edge of the counter for support.

Craig waited for an uncertain moment, and then she

heard him sigh. "Laurie, the last thing I want to do is force myself on you," he said, "but a moment ago I was under the distinct impression that you wanted the same thing I did."

The words made Laurie's knuckles whiten on the edge of the counter. What he wanted, she told herself, was nothing more than to amuse himself with a willing body—the way he had with so many other willing bodies.

But he was right about her actions. Despite all her resolve, she had given him the impression that she was as eager for casual dalliance as he.

Laurie clenched her fist. But, then, hadn't it been the skill of Craig's lovemaking that had swept her along on a flood of unaccustomed passion? If she had known how dangerous it was going to be, she never would have allowed him into her apartment. However, she wasn't going to stand here and explain to him that his touch had prevented her from thinking rationally.

"Please leave," she repeated.

This time, to her relief, Craig didn't argue. Without another word of protest, he turned on his heels. A moment later she heard the apartment door close very quietly behind him.

CHAPTER FOUR

Laurie had set her alarm for eight the next morning so that she could plan the talk she had promised to give in Sandy's weight control seminar. But long before the buzzer sounded, she reached over and shut the mechanism off. She was wide-awake. In fact, it seemed as though she had spent most of the night watching the reflected light from passing cars slide along the length of her ceiling.

Thoughts of Craig had kept her from shutting her eyes for more than a few minutes at a time.

She was resentful of him and angry at herself for turning to mush in his hands. How would someone with more experience have kept him at bay in the kitchen? she wondered. Probably by defusing his advances with humor. But she had been too affected by his nearness to handle herself with that much aplomb. She'd behaved like a nervous adolescent instead of the mature woman she was. But was that really her fault? she asked herself. In every other area of her life she had learned to cope effectively.

However, when it came to man-woman encounters, she was a beginner. And the problem was magnified by her complicated history with Craig. Why had she let her sister talk her into going out with him? It had been a big mistake. *If I had just met the man,* she mused, with a touch of regret, *there wouldn't really be a problem.* She could take his attraction to her at face value. But she knew that never in his wildest dreams would he have tried to seduce her a year ago. That central fact made all the difference. The thought made her pound her fists against the mattress in frustration.

What's more, her frustration wasn't just mental. It was physical as well. The evening with Craig had aroused longings and needs that she had no idea how to cope with. All the sensitive places in her body had seemed to burn with newly awakened fires, and when she'd rolled over onto her stomach, it had been as if his hands, not the mattress, were pressed against her tingling breasts.

After swinging her legs over the side of the bed, she got up and peered out the window. Bright sunshine had successfully challenged the early-morning gray of the sky. Another nice day was in store, she thought. And she was going to make sure she took advantage of it instead of wasting time thinking about Craig Lawson. But before she could do that, she'd have to take care of this obligation to Sandy. The realization was enough to make her put aside her preoccupation with last night, and resolutely she headed for a cold shower. She owed it to her sister to do a good job.

What's more, the subject was one that deserved her best efforts.

Two hours later, as she strolled across the sprawling university campus, Laurie couldn't help thinking back on her own student days. Although academically her experience here had been a very good one, socially she'd felt like a failure. Most of that, she now admitted, had been because of her weight problem. What if there'd been a seminar like the one Sandy was leading? Would she have signed up for it? And would it have helped? How different her life might have been if she'd gotten control of her problem earlier. That was what she was going to tell the kids, she resolved as she entered the health service building where the session was scheduled.

The group of ten young people who were waiting in room 301 looked up nervously when she crossed the threshold.

"Here's our guest speaker and shining example," Sandy exclaimed from her perch on top of the desk facing the semicircle of chairs. Pushing herself up, she gestured her sister to the center of the room.

"This is Laurie DiMaria," she explained. "As you look at her, it's hard to believe she was ever anything but slim and trim. But I happen to know she worked hard over the past year to lose more than forty pounds. And she's told me that she intends to keep it off."

Laurie could see the group studying her curiously.

"Yes, it's true," she admitted. "And what I did, you can do, too," she added.

In the next forty-five minutes she went on to give a presentation that was half carefully prepared health and nutritional information and half pep talk.

When she was finished, eager hands went up all over the room, and just as at the Russel Corporation earlier that week, she was assailed by a barrage of questions.

"I've always used food as a reward," one girl said. "How do you give yourself a treat without spoiling your diet?"

"Sometimes I save up for a dress that I like. Or maybe I make an appointment at the beauty shop for a facial or a manicure that I wouldn't ordinarily indulge in."

"Did you ever attach a picture of a pig to the refrigerator door?" someone else asked.

Laurie laughed. "No, I've never done that. But it sounds like a very good strategy."

Her enthusiasm seemed to touch off a corresponding spark in the students. When the session broke up, she felt as though she might have made a real difference. To emphasize the point, a slightly pudgy young man approached her as she was putting away her notes.

"I'm Buddy Parks," he said a bit shyly. "Ms. Campana told us you work at the Russel Corporation."

"That's right."

"I'm a co-op there—you know, I go to school half-time and work the other half. Anyway, I was wondering if you'd be willing to give me some advice."

Laurie smiled encouragingly. "What can I help you with?"

"Well, I really want to lose twenty pounds. But it's hard to do it eating in the company cafeteria at lunch."

"I know what you mean," Laurie said. It seemed to specialize in fat and starch.

"Mostly I try to stick with the salad bar. Is that okay?" he asked, obviously expecting her approval.

"Only if you pick the right things," Laurie answered.

He looked startled. "I thought salad was about as nonfattening as you could get."

"It is—if you stay away from the potato salad and go light on the bacon bits, the shredded cheddar, chick-peas, and sunflower seeds. And use the low-cal dressing."

"Gee, I never thought about that. But I guess you're right," he said reluctantly.

Laurie could see he wasn't happy about skimping on some of the goodies she'd mentioned. Grinning, she patted him on the back. "It's hard at first. But after a while you get used to it. And you even get to like it," she said encouragingly. Then an idea struck her. "Say, did you know the Russel Corporation has a terrific gym for its employees? I'll

58

bet you could use it, even though you're part-time. Did you know physical activity is a great appetite depressant, and it works off calories, too?"

That led into another five minutes of discussion with the young man about the virtues of physical fitness and keeping the body in shape by working out regularly.

When Buddy was finally out the door, Sandy turned to her sister with a grin. "You seemed to have really hit it off with those kids. And your talk was great. I'm just sorry we took up so much of your Saturday."

Laurie touched her sister's shoulder warmly. "Think nothing of it. I enjoyed it, and I even managed to inspire myself. Actually I'm going to follow my own advice. Want to try the salad bar in the cafeteria and then head over to the gym?"

"I'd love to have lunch with you, but I can't stay for the workout in the gym. I promised the kids a trip to the farmer's market. But, after your talk I think I'll make strawberries our main treat."

Laurie turned away quickly. The mention of the lush red fruit brought back memories of last night's fiasco with Craig. And, if the truth be known, that was one of the reasons she'd decided to spend the afternoon working off her frustration on a racquetball court.

After a light lunch Sandy dropped her sister at the gym the Russel Corporation maintained for its employees. Quickly Laurie changed into a pair of navy shorts and a white knit pullover. She'd bought the outfit just a few days before, so it still felt crisp and new. Sitting on one of the wooden benches, she pulled on her thick cotton socklets and indoor court shoes and then fished a rubber band from her purse. Having pulled her long hair into a ponytail, she secured it tightly and then surveyed her image in the mirror.

Was that trim, athletic-looking brunette really her? she asked herself with a small, private grin. Sometimes she still had trouble believing it. The year before she would have considered a fast game of jacks with her niece more than adequate exercise. Now she made sure she jogged, swam, or played racquetball at least three or four times a week.

At the desk she signed onto the last remaining free court and then headed down the green-carpeted corridor. She hadn't been kidding Buddy when she'd extolled the virtues of the gym. The Russel Corporation had gone all out when it had been built. Besides the luxurious carpeting, it had a fully equipped weight room, separate saunas for men and women, and an almost sinfully decadent whirlpool with potted palms and hanging plants. The facility was a great success with the employees—particularly the men. Craig, she knew, used it regularly to keep in shape. But that wasn't his only motive for coming here. Suddenly she remembered that he had once laughingly told her that the whirlpool was an excellent place to meet girls. The warm, swirling waters put them in a receptive mood. And because of the skimpy bathing suits they wore, you didn't have to guess about what you were getting.

The thought made her clench her jaw and hit her fist against the taut mesh of her racquet. It was just one more reminder of Craig Lawson's attitude toward women. He really saw them only when they met his standards for good looks.

Pushing open the heavy door of the court, she stalked inside. Without bothering to go through her usual stretching and warming-up routine, she bounced the blue rubber ball on the wood floor in front of her and then slammed it against the pockmarked wall at the opposite end of the court. When the ball shot back, she dashed across the court to position herself correctly for another healthy slam. Usually when she practiced by herself this way, she let some of the balls go by, since playing alone was so strenuous. But this morning she was in an aggressive mood. Charging back and forth across the court, she made sure she got every shot, even if she had to jump or stretch to connect with the ball.

It was the wrong strategy for someone who hadn't bothered to warm up. She hadn't been at it for more than a few minutes when she lunged to the side for a difficult backhand and felt a shooting pain in her thigh. For a moment she leaned against the wall, breathing heavily.

It's nothing, she assured herself. *I can probably work it out.* Doggedly she began to walk slowly around the court. And after a few laps the pain did recede so that she could resume a somewhat less strenuous practice session.

But the next time she dived for the ball, pain coursed through her thigh with such sharpness that the impact almost brought her down to the floor. Muttering a not very ladylike oath under her breath, she let the ball go by. *I should have quit while I was ahead,* she told herself, taking a step toward the door. It was now almost impossible to put any weight on the injured limb, and she knew she had definitely made a mistake to push herself.

When she got outside, she could barely hobble down the hall and wondered how in the world she was going to make it back to her apartment building. It was a long walk under ordinary circumstances, but crippled as she was, it was going to be impossible. Maybe Sandy would be able to pick her up again, she thought hopefully before remembering that her sister was off to the farmer's market. Knowing Sandy, she might be gone for several hours.

Sighing, Laurie leaned against the cinder block wall to take the pressure off her leg. She was almost at the seating

61

area at the end of the corridor where she could rest awhile and figure out what to do.

Repressing a wince of pain at each step, she inched toward the chairs. Just then she felt a strong hand on her arm. "What's wrong?" a deep familiar voice asked.

Laurie turned and found herself looking up into Craig's questioning green eyes. Since coming back to work, she had half expected to run into him at the athletic club, but why did it have to be now? she wondered.

"It's really nothing," she said, minimizing the pain. "I just pulled something."

But Craig wasn't buying her offhand disclaimer. "I watched you take a couple of steps," he observed. "You can barely put any weight on that leg. And I doubt that you can drive yourself home."

"It doesn't matter; I don't have my car here," she admitted, resignedly allowing Craig to lower her onto one of the plastic upholstered seats. The touch of his hard fingers on her flushed skin was a vivid reminder of how they'd parted the night before, and she couldn't quite meet his eyes.

"That settles it. I'll drive you," he was saying. "Just let me change my clothes, and I'll be right back."

"You don't . . ." Laurie started to protest. But he was already striding off toward the men's dressing room. As she watched, she could see that his white shorts and T-shirt were still crisp. He obviously hadn't even started his workout yet.

Despite herself, she couldn't keep her eyes from drifting below the edge of his jogging shorts to the firm thickness of his muscled thighs. She remembered what he'd told her the evening before about being a scrawny kid. There was nothing scrawny about him now. Hard work had molded his body into that of an athlete. When he'd told her about picking up women at the club, he'd joked about being able to see exactly what he was getting. But that worked both ways. Probably the women here were just as pleased by what they saw when they looked at him. Probably, she admitted to herself, they were interested in picking him up, too. And she really couldn't blame him for that.

Almost as soon as Craig disappeared through the door to the men's locker room, another scantily clad young man stepped out. Without realizing what she was doing, Laurie had been staring at the closed door. Suddenly, to her chagrin, she found her gaze locked with the frankly interested one of a stranger. Flushing with embarrassment, she looked away and focused on one of the racquetball games in progress behind the glass-walled courts that lined the lounge area. But it was too late. She'd already caught the other man's attention. In less than a minute he was drawing up a seat beside her and introducing himself as Jerry Carmichael.

When Craig finally returned, she was carrying on a stilted conversation that, on her part, consisted mainly of mumbled replies to Jerry's persistent attempts to get chummy. Taking in the situation, Craig strode to her side and put a proprietary arm on her shoulder.

"Didn't keep you waiting too long, did I?"

Laurie shook her head, and Jerry took his cue from Craig's unwelcoming expression.

"Well, guess I'd better see when the next exercise class starts. See you around," he said as he got up to leave.

"Sure," Laurie answered for the sake of politeness, and then looked up to see that Craig's green eyes had iced over.

"Come on. Let's get out of here," he muttered, reaching out and starting to pull her to her feet. But her wince of pain made him remember what had occasioned their departure in the first place. "Oh, Laurie, I'm sorry," he said, his eyes once more warm with concern. "Do you want me to carry you to the car?"

Laurie was horrified by the prospect. People were already staring at the way he had put his arm around her waist and forced her weight onto his shoulder. She was going to feel a lot more conspicuous if he picked her up. "I think I can manage," she insisted. "But someone's going to have to get my pocketbook out of the ladies' locker room."

That mission was accomplished easily enough by one of the club's attendants. But afterward getting out to the parking lot turned into a long, slow operation. By the time she was settled in the bucket seat of his sports car her face was pale.

"I should have gotten some ice for you," Craig thought aloud as he slipped behind the wheel. "Do you have some left in your freezer, or should we stop?"

Laurie was having trouble concentrating on his words. "Yes, I mean no, you don't have to stop," she replied, leaning back against the leather seat and closing her eyes.

It wasn't until she felt the car slow in front of her building that she looked up.

"I'll leave you on the bench by the door," Craig said as he helped her out. "As soon as I've parked the car, I'll be right back."

When he pulled away, she stubbornly ignored his instructions and tried to make it to the elevators on her own.

"What the hell do you think you're doing?" Craig demanded when he found her leaning against the wall, her face ashen. At that moment the door opened. Before she could protest, he swept her up into his arms and, like the hero of a romantic historical movie, carried her inside.

"Put me down," Laurie said insistently.

But Craig simply pushed the button to her floor and continued to hold her firmly while their car moved swiftly upward.

Thank God the elevator was empty, Laurie thought. What would someone who saw them think?

Unfortunately her fear was realized when the door slid open at the third floor and she found herself staring into the eyes of a startled-looking Art Frazier. Carrying a basket of laundry, he was obviously headed for the washing machines in the basement. When he took in the sight of Laurie in Craig's arms, his blond eyebrows shot upward. "Laurie, what . . ." he started to exclaim. At that moment the door slid closed, and the elevator resumed its upward journey.

"Another acquaintance of yours?" Craig inquired sweetly, putting the emphasis on the noun. "You seem to have met a lot of men in the short time you've been back."

Laurie glared at him. She was feeling even more like a fool now. There was no good way to answer his question, so she simply ignored it. "Will you please put me down?"

"Not until we get your leg taken care of."

The determination in his voice made Laurie try a different tack. "Aren't you afraid of hurting yourself? I'm not exactly a featherweight."

Craig grinned wolfishly down into her face, and she couldn't help being intensely aware of their physical contact. Shifting her body slightly in his arms, he pulled her even more tightly against the broad expanse of his chest. "Oh, but that's exactly what you are. You don't weigh anything. I could carry you in my arms all day."

Laurie blinked and then, unable to resist baiting him, laughed hollowly.

"What's so funny?" he demanded as the metal doors whooshed open on her floor and he stepped out into the hall.

"I know damn well you wouldn't have said that a year

ago," she said challengingly. "In fact, by now you would have been too winded to say anything."

Craig stared at her in consternation, and Laurie found herself taking a perverse satisfaction in knowing that he was once again having a hard time connecting the fragile young woman he held in his arms with the overweight companion she'd been before. "I could have carried you then, too," he finally muttered as he strode down the corridor and stopped in front of her door. "Now, where are your keys?"

After fumbling in her bag, Laurie handed them over. A moment later Craig was depositing her on the couch in the living room.

"I'm going to need a towel to wrap the ice," he informed her. "Where do you keep them?"

Laurie would have liked to tell him to leave now that he'd gotten her safely to her apartment. But it was obvious that he had no intention of doing that just yet.

"In the linen closet at the end of the hall," she said with a sigh. But the words were no sooner out of her mouth than she remembered that the shelves of that closet contained more than towels. Since she did not yet have a chest of drawers in the bedroom, she had stored her underwear there. What's more, she'd splurged when she'd bought it, taking delight in wispy silks and laces in French-cut styles. It was possible that he might simply grab a towel and not see the stacks of sensual lingerie, she thought hopefully. But he didn't reappear instantly, so she knew that something besides the towels was holding his attention.

When he came back into the room, he didn't say a word. But a smile hovered around the corners of his mouth.

"You have very nice towels," he called from the kitchen as he opened the refrigerator door and pulled out an ice tray.

Yes, very nice, he thought as he sealed the cubes in a plastic bag and then wrapped the bag in thick blue terry. They both knew that it wasn't visions of towels dancing through his mind at the moment. In fact, he was amusing himself by picturing Laurie in the black lace push-up bra and scanty silk panties he couldn't help having noticed in her linen closet. Now that he knew what was beneath those conservative business suits she wore, his little fantasies about her were going to be a lot more detailed.

Did she wear lacy wisps like that under her racquetball outfits, too? he wondered. But maybe he'd better not pursue that line of thought. He was here because Laurie had hurt herself. Yet it was impossible to keep his mind strictly on her health as he knelt on the floor in front of her.

"Now just exactly where does it hurt?" he asked, trying to keep his tone impersonal.

When Laurie refused to look at him, it was apparent that her mind had to be running along the same lines as his. "My thigh," she mumbled, reaching out for the towel-wrapped ice and encountering his hand instead.

Craig's eyes brightened. "That's a very vulnerable area," he informed her, applying the ice pack to the outside of the injured limb.

"That's not the right place. It's the inside"—Laurie bit the words out—"and I'd rather do it myself."

Craig did his best to look stern. Although he couldn't help enjoying the opportunity this was giving him to touch Laurie intimately, he did know that the right first aid could make all the difference in the speed of her recovery. "Now this is no time for modesty," he said admonishingly. "It sounds as if you've pulled a tendon. And if we don't get ice on it right away, you could be heading for tendinitis."

"Tendinitis?" Laurie said doubtfully.

"Yes. I had it myself a few years ago, and it's no joke. I had a macho fantasy that I could work through the pain of an injury like yours. Instead, I wound up nursing a bad arm for months."

Laurie nodded, applying the ice pack. "But I can't sit here all afternoon," she pointed out.

"If I were you, I'd stay off that leg for the rest of the weekend," Craig said, "but today is particularly important."

"There are things I have to do," Laurie said. And one of them, she realized, was to visit the bathroom. But she certainly wasn't going to tell Craig *that.*

"Like what?" he shot back.

"Um, like do a load of wash, fix lunch . . ." Her voice trailed off.

"As for the laundry, I can't believe you're in need of underwear, judging from the X-rated stash I found in your linen closet." Ignoring her exclamation, he plowed on. "And I'll do your cooking today. So you don't have any excuse to get up after all."

For a moment Laurie was stymied by his persistence. The last thing she wanted was a bright-eyed Craig Lawson hanging around her apartment all day. Then she had an idea. "Look, I think I'd like to lie down for a while. If you'll just help me into my bedroom, you can go home."

Craig crossed his arms. "You're not taking this seriously enough. I'll *carry* you into the bedroom. But you're not getting rid of me that easily."

Laurie's eyebrows shot up.

"I mean, while you're taking your nap, I'll do some grocery shopping. When you wake up, Chef Lawson will have fixed some dinner."

"Really, you don't have to do that," Laurie said.

Once more Craig ignored her protests. "I know I don't have to," he said, and then added more softly, "But I want to." Without waiting for a reply, he once again swept her up into his arms and carried her down the hall.

CHAPTER FIVE

Alone at last, Laurie thought, looking at the door Craig had quietly closed behind him. Waiting until his steps receded down the hall, she pushed herself to a sitting position on the futon. Craig was probably right. She should try to keep off the leg. Maybe she could slide along the floor on her bottom, she thought. Lucky the apartment's new carpeting meant she didn't have to worry about picking up a splinter, she told herself as she eased off the futon onto the floor and began to pull herself toward the bathroom on her bottom. A wry smile twisted the corners of her mouth. She could just imagine Craig's enthusiasm if he had to put ice on that particular area.

A few minutes later, feeling much more ready for a nap, she made her snaillike way back to the futon and collapsed. She had told Craig she wanted to lie down. But she hadn't realized how much truth was in her words. The strain of her injury plus her lack of sleep last night had taken their toll. She had only to close her eyes to drift off into a deep sleep.

After checking out the groceries in the kitchen and fixing himself a cup of coffee, Craig glanced at his watch. It had been twenty minutes since he'd left Laurie in her bedroom, and she'd looked pale when he'd helped her onto that damn silly futon. Maybe he should see how she was doing.

Tiptoeing down the hall, he listened at the closed door. "Laurie," he murmured, and, when there was no answer, turned the knob and quietly pushed the door open. Across the room, snuggled in a quilt, Laurie lay very still. She presented an appealing picture with her dark lashes feathering silky shadows on the smooth olive skin of her cheeks. Her gym shoes were on the floor beside her futon, and Craig grimaced as he looked again at the patterned cushion she was sleeping on. How anyone could actually rest, let alone get a good night's sleep, on such a narrow, flimsy mattress was beyond him. Yet she was obviously quite comfortable. Her year in Japan seemed to have equipped her with a lot of new skills. Before she left, he had assumed this woman held no surprises for him. Now she was like a will-o'-the-wisp, tantalizing and intriguing him. He had thought he had her in his grasp last night. But she had slipped away again.

As he watched, she stirred slightly in her sleep, her hand coming up to push a wayward strand of raven hair away from her cheek. Craig's fingers closed around the doorjamb. It took a considerable amount of willpower to keep himself from tiptoeing across the room and kneeling down to take her in his arms and kiss her closed eyelids.

But that was out of the question. If she'd spent the kind of restless night he had after their frustrating date, she needed her rest. Closing the door firmly but quietly, he made his way back to the kitchen, where he wrote a note explaining that he was going shopping. He was about to leave it on the kitchen counter when he stopped and shook his head. Instead, he added a sentence: "Stay where you are." Then he put the paper outside her bedroom door.

After picking up Laurie's keys from where he'd dropped them, he left the apartment and went down to his car. Just a few blocks away there was a grocery store where he could

71

get anything he needed. What would Laurie like for dinner? he wondered. The question preoccupied him all the way to the market. Even when he was inside pushing a cart down the aisle, he was unsure.

Did she like seafood? His easy crab-stuffed flounder was usually a success. And although it tasted rich, he knew it was surprisingly low in calories. From their dinner last night, he knew she'd appreciate that.

Once the decision had been made, he quickly picked up the seafood, along with the makings of a simple salad and some beautiful fresh California asparagus. He was tempted to top his purchases off with cheesecake. But Laurie probably wouldn't go for that. Instead, he stopped in a nearby liquor store and bought some rum, brandy, and a light white wine.

As he stowed his packages in the trunk, he realized he was humming. The shopping expedition had put him in a good mood, which was unusual since he didn't normally enjoy spending a Saturday afternoon at the supermarket. Somehow, doing it for Laurie made all the difference. Since the last acrimonious days of his marriage he'd deliberately avoided taking responsibility for others and had grown accustomed to thinking primarily about his own needs. It had been partly a defensive reaction, but it had become such a habit that he was now surprised at how much pleasure he was getting out of the simple services he had been performing for Laurie. Probably if he'd left her alone with this leg injury, her dinner would have been a cup of yogurt. But he was going to make sure she had something a lot better. And he was looking forward to sharing the meal as well as her stimulating company.

He was still humming when he carried his purchases into the kitchen and set about his preparations for dinner. The nice thing about the main course was that he could prepare it ahead of time and refrigerate it. As he washed the greens for the salad, he began thinking about the relationship he was trying to establish with Laurie. Here in the kitchen last night she had responded to him with all the sensuality he had suspected was hidden behind her conservative workday exterior. She was attracted to him; he was certain of that. Still, when her mind, not her body, was in control, she was trying to hold him at arm's length.

What accounted for it? he wondered. They'd always liked each other, and he'd thought they could build a more intimate bond on that. Now he wasn't sure of anything. Laurie seemed to be wary of him in a way she never had been before. Could it be her lack of experience? He suspected she hadn't dated very much. Could she be a virgin? The thought made his hands pause over the lettuce leaves he was tearing. The idea startled him. After all, virgins were as scarce as hen's teeth these days. But Laurie was both shy and sensitive. She wouldn't have settled for a casual affair, he suspected. And she probably hadn't dated much before her startling transformation anyway.

If he was guessing right, then no wonder she was skittish. The realization sent a flood of warmth through him, and he stared down at the dewy green leaves in the colander without seeing them.

All at once it came to him: Laurie DiMaria was everything he had always wanted in a woman. That must be why, like an overeager kid, he had been pushing things too fast.

But the best things in life were worth waiting for. *Take it more slowly,* he told himself. *Laurie's attracted to you, or she wouldn't have been so upset last night.*

He still wanted very much to be her lover. But now he could see that the role carried responsibilities as well as

73

pleasures. When the time came, he vowed, he would be caring and tender with her so that she would never regret her first experience.

The sound of a whirring blender wakened Laurie. For a moment she lay on her futon in confusion. What was she doing here in the middle of the day, and who was in her kitchen? Then she remembered, and her head swiveled sharply toward the door. That was Craig out there. What was he mixing up? He had said he would fix dinner, and apparently he was fulfilling his promise.

Struggling to a sitting position, she realized she was still wearing her racquetball outfit. But now the crisp cotton was crumpled, and she felt the need to put on something fresh. What's more, she didn't want to face Craig again in such an abbreviated costume. Undoubtedly, if she came out in shorts, he'd try to put another ice pack on her leg, and she didn't want to repeat that little scene.

In her closet was a long, flowing kaftan in a deep ruby velvet. That ought to serve as a good cover-up, she thought. As she made her way to the closet, she realized that her thigh was still tender and slightly swollen. Probably she would do well to continue following Craig's advice and keep off that leg as much as possible. Should she call him to help her to the living room? she wondered as she zipped up the floor-length garment. No, she was damned if she would let him carry her down the hall again.

Somehow she managed to make it out to the living room without putting too much strain on the leg or alerting Craig. When she had sunk down on the couch so that she could observe the activities in the kitchen, she could see why. He seemed to be totally absorbed by his dinner preparations. What's more, he was humming softly as he moved between

74

the stove and the refrigerator. She couldn't help smiling. She'd had no idea that he was so much at home in a kitchen.

Finally, she couldn't help commenting on the fact. "You weren't kidding when you called yourself Chef Lawson."

Craig was so startled by the unexpected sound of her voice that he almost dropped the salad bowl. "How did you get out here?" he asked challengingly. "You were supposed to call me when you were ready to get up."

"Oh, I thought it was time I started doing something for myself," she answered. "In fact, is there any way I can help with dinner?"

"No. I want you to be a lady of leisure this evening, so just stay where you are and relax." As he spoke, he opened the oven door. "Let me just get the main course out of the way, and I'll bring you out a drink." Turning back to the refrigerator, he pulled out the blender container. It was full of a pink frothy concoction.

"That looks like one of my fruit shakes," she blurted out, and then wished she'd kept her mouth shut. Why remind either one of them of last night's debacle?

But Craig simply shook his head and smiled serenely. "Similar, but it does have some rum in it. However, I did take a page from your book and cut the usual sugar." As he spoke, he poured the mixture into two glasses. Before carrying them out to the living room, he unfolded a metal tray stand and set it down in front of her.

"Where did that come from?" she asked in amazement.

Craig shrugged. "I picked up a couple at the shopping center. I thought they'd be good to put the drinks on. That way you don't have to keep leaning over to get yours off the floor."

Laurie couldn't keep from staring at him. When he'd first volunteered to help her back to her apartment, she'd half suspected that it was just a ploy to get her alone again. But surely this was much more than that. In fact, such thoughtfulness both surprised and touched her. Had Craig always been this considerate of her welfare? she wondered. Up to now she'd been recalling only his inability to see her as anything but a pal. Now she remembered what a good friend he really had been and reproached herself for her unfairness. There had been the time when he'd found her in the parking lot with an immobilized car, waited with her for a mechanic, and then driven her home when the car had had to be serviced overnight. Or what about the time she'd dropped all the change out of her wallet in the cafeteria line? While other people had laughed at her predicament, Craig had got down on the floor and helped her pick up the runaway dimes and pennies.

The memories made her smile warmly as he brought their drinks in from the kitchen. When he saw the welcoming look on her face, Craig's expression brightened.

"You seem to be feeling a lot better," he observed, handing her a tumbler of the frosty pink liquid. "Penny for your thoughts," he added.

Laurie took a sip and then nodded appreciatively. "This is really good—and not too heavy on the rum either."

Craig grinned. "Yes, but when I asked what you were thinking, you hadn't tasted it yet. So come on, stop avoiding the question. What's brought that sparkle to your big brown eyes?"

"Oh, I was just thinking about when you first came to Russel," she said. "You know, the whole secretarial pool was buzzing about what a catch you were—and not just for the corporation. All that talk made me think you were going to be the self-centered type, intent on advancement in the company and hard to work for."

Craig raised an eyebrow.

"But you weren't really that way," Laurie added hastily.

He looked at her thoughtfully. "I'm glad you have pleasant memories of those early days. I know I do." He paused, his brow furrowing slightly. "But there are things I wish I'd done differently, things I was blind to . . . you know, Laurie," he started to admit.

Suspecting what he might be going to say, she quickly cut him off and changed the subject. "What are we having for dinner?" she asked. "It's beginning to smell awfully good."

Craig gave her a quizzical look. "You must be smelling the crab-stuffed flounder," he said, and then ran through the menu he'd selected.

Laurie's jaw dropped. "My goodness, that all sounds wonderful. Maybe I should hurt my leg more often."

"Oh, you don't have to do anything that drastic," Craig said as he got up to put dinner on the table. Laurie felt a little pang of guilt. It wasn't like her to sit by and let someone else do all the work. But he had ordered her to stay where she was. And she knew her leg really did need the rest. So why not enjoy the pampering?

When everything was ready, Craig effortlessly scooped her up into his arms, and suddenly she found her face very close to his strongly chiseled masculine features. "I'd enjoy fixing dinner for you even if you weren't injured," he murmured huskily, looking down into her wide brown eyes.

Laurie was speechless. But he only smiled at her blushing confusion and carried her into the kitchen, where he sat her down gently on a chair.

Dinner was every bit as good as Craig had advertised. What's more, he had obviously given some thought to making the menu light as well as delicious. He hadn't smothered the asparagus in a heavy sauce, and Laurie was able to eat the flavorful crab stuffing without feeling guilty.

"You'll have to give me this recipe," she commented as she forked up the last of her entrée. It was the kind of thing she might have said to her sister. The realization made her giggle. It seemed so strange to be asking someone as thoroughly masculine as Craig Lawson for his cooking secrets.

"What's so funny?" he demanded as he stood up to clear the table.

When she explained, he only guffawed. "Now who's a chauvinist? Aren't you forgetting that most of the world's great chefs are men? Actually," he went on, "it sounds as if you have a great relationship with your sister. And I'm a bit jealous."

"Jealous?" Laurie gave him a questioning look.

"Yes. I guess there was so much squabbling between the kids in my family that none of us is very close. In fact, we never had a very close family. I feel as if I've been on my own most of my life."

"In what sense?" Laurie asked. Because she'd come from such a warm and loving home, she found it difficult to empathize with his feelings.

"Well, how would you like to have been the kid whose parents never went to any of the school plays—even when you had a leading role? Or the one who never went on the school trips because they were too expensive? If it hadn't been for scholarships and summer jobs, I never would have made it through college," he said. "My parents were too busy struggling to make ends meet to give us any real emotional support. I guess I grew up thinking that if anyone was going to stand up for number one, it had to be me."

He paused for a moment. "After my divorce I told myself

78

I liked it that way. But lately I've begun to wonder if I've been missing something."

She was trying to think how to answer that revealing statement when she realized that he was stacking all the plates in the dishwasher. "Oh, listen, you cooked dinner. Why don't you leave that for me to do later?" Laurie protested.

"Remember what I said about being a lady of leisure? Well, I meant it," he asserted, obviously intent on bringing the conversation back to a lighter note. As he talked, he made short work of the remaining dishes. When the kitchen was neat and clean, he poured their coffee and brandy. "Why don't we have this out in the living room?"

Automatically Laurie pushed back her chair and stood up. She had momentarily forgotten all about her sore leg. But the second she put pressure on it, the pain returned, and she winced visibly.

Quickly having put down the cups, Craig once more swung her into his arms. "See, you need someone to watch over you," he whispered in her ear as he carried her back to the other room. "You've been neglecting Dr. Lawson's prescription for that sore leg."

"You don't mean you want to put an ice pack on it now?" Laurie said protestingly.

"Well, maybe not right this minute. But you really should ice it down again after we've finished our coffee."

He was standing in front of the couch now, cradling her against his chest, and she waited for him to set her down. It had been twilight when they'd started dinner, but now the living room was dark and shadowy. The lack of light created an intimacy that hadn't been there before. She knew the man who held her in his muscular arms felt it as strongly as she. Instead of lowering her to the couch, one of his hands shifted from under her knee to close around her ankle.

"You're so delicately made," he murmured. As he spoke, he ran his finger around the bone structure at the top of her foot, caressing the sensitive hollows and ridges that he found there.

As his hand moved over her skin, Laurie stared up into his face as though mesmerized. Her ankles and feet were delicate, she knew. She had always been rather vain about them even when she hadn't had much else to be vain about. But she'd never before thought of them as an erogenous zone. Now, as Craig's warm fingers continued their random caressing pattern, she was beginning to realize how sensitive they were. The sensations were so delicious that she found herself relaxing against his chest and closing her eyes. Why did she have to make everything so complicated between Craig and herself? she wondered. Had she been erecting artificial barriers between them by doubting his sincerity? When you brought everything down to this level, their relationship didn't seem complicated at all. He appeared to be feeling the same thing. For a long moment he rested his cheek against the top of her head. Then, sighing, he slowly lowered her to the couch.

"I'd better go bring in our coffee," he said in a husky voice.

"Yes," she said in a tone almost as husky as his. As she waited for him to return, she leaned back against the couch cushions, feeling warm and contented—and something else, too. Yet beneath it all there was still a hesitancy about where this second evening alone with Craig might be leading. As if to emphasize her apprehension, she heard him turn on the radio in the kitchen. He seemed to know which station he wanted, and in seconds soft, romantic music was drifting toward her.

"Don't you want to put the overhead light on?" she asked when he came back into the room.

"No, I like it this way," he said as he put their cups down on the tray stand. "There's enough light coming from the kitchen so that we can see," he added as he joined her on the sofa.

She supposed he was right and thought she might sound silly to protest. But somehow the room would have seemed safer if it were a little brighter. Craig leaned forward and handed her a coffee cup.

"It's delicious," she murmured after taking a sip. "I've never had this before. What's in it?"

"It's a walnut-flavored liqueur. I think it's particularly good in coffee."

"Good? It's wonderful! In fact, it tastes almost sinful."

He cocked his head. "I'm curious. Why are you equating goodness with sin?"

For a moment Laurie was startled. "Am I? I guess you're right. Maybe I was thinking about my family again. If my mother had any fault, it was providing us with too much of a good thing—at least when it came to mealtimes and snacks. She admired fat babies and plump little girls." Laurie paused and ran a finger around the rim of her coffee cup. "Self-restraint was not something I learned at my mother's table. So I've had to teach it to myself."

Over the rim of his cup Craig studied the beautiful but insecure woman opposite him for a moment. "Do you ever wonder if you might not be overcompensating?"

"What do you mean?"

Craig set their cups down. "Just because you've developed an iron will where food is concerned doesn't mean you should deny yourself other pleasures. I mean, you're always so serious, Laurie. You've got to unbend a little. There are plenty of things in life you can enjoy without feeling guilty."

"But I do," she said protestingly. "There *are* lots of things I enjoy."

"Like what?"

The question was so direct that for an embarrassing moment her mind went blank. "I enjoy my job for one thing," she finally said.

"Surely you can do better than that," Craig replied.

He was right, she realized. That was a pretty pat answer. "I enjoy being independent and having my own apartment. Jogging on a fine morning is a pleasure to me. And there are lots of other things, like taking my sister's kids out for an afternoon or just a quiet evening with good music and a good book."

Craig reached out to take her hand. "But, Laurie, listen to yourself. Except for your sister's kids, everything you've mentioned so far is something you do alone. Don't you think it's time you learned to find pleasure with someone else?"

As he spoke, he raised the palm of her hand to his mouth and pressed a soft kiss into it. The feel of his lips against the sensitive skin did strange things to Laurie's insides. Little tremors of excitement began to awaken, growing and spreading deliciously through her system, while at the same time her chest constricted and her large brown eyes widened.

Her fingers quivered slightly in his, but he didn't release them. Instead, he spread her small hand flat in the cradle of his large one and gazed down at it.

"Are you reading my palm?" she inquired.

"Yes."

"What do you see?"

He smiled into her face and then returned his gaze to her hand. "I see a long lifeline, but it's the love line that interests me."

Laurie knew he was teasing her, but she couldn't resist asking, "What's so fascinating about the love line?"

"It gets started rather late, but once under way, it's very strong and lasts just as long as your lifeline." He turned his handsome head and met her eyes again. "Do you know what that means?"

Like a small, hypnotized animal quivering with anticipation, Laurie was mute. But her large dark eyes told Craig everything he wanted to know.

"It means you're going to discover your passionate nature very soon," he murmured. She had no time to consider what he really meant by those words. As he spoke, his arms slipped around Laurie's waist, and his head bent toward hers.

While she had been asleep, he had vowed to take things more slowly with her. But now that he had her in his arms, it was impossible to draw back. All he could think about was the delicate feminine scent of her skin, the soft brush of her hair against his cheek, and the way her slender body felt against his.

Laurie, too, was being swept away by the same tide of sensation, her doubts about Craig's motives forgotten for the moment. When his lips began to brush gently against her mouth, she trembled uncontrollably with a wild mixture of uncertainty and desire. She wanted to be close to Craig, to feel his strong arms wrapped around her body and his mouth kissing hers. At the same time, like a child facing the unknown, she was afraid. Craig was an experienced lover. Even she could recognize his assured expertise as he shifted his attention from her quivering mouth and began to drop light caresses along her hairline and then the lobe of her ear. When he compared her to the other women he'd held in his arms, would he not find her boring and inadequate?

But as his lips roamed over her face and his arms stroked her body into a yielding compliance, these thoughts were soon pushed far to the back of Laurie's befogged mind. She was too lost in the new sensations he was arousing to fret long over her lack of expertise.

"You're so very lovely," he whispered huskily before nipping lightly at her earlobe. "I'd like to kiss every delicious inch of you."

"Craig," she muttered weakly, "you shouldn't . . ." But there was no conviction in her voice, and even as she issued the mild protest, she was tipping her head back so that he could more easily graze over the sensitive line of her jaw and down the column of her warm throat. In a moment his mouth had found the throbbing hollow, and as he pressed his lips into it, Laurie couldn't hold back a moan of pleasure.

"That's it," he told her, lowering her body back against the couch cushions and stretching out his long, hard length next to her. "Just relax, and let me love you. You don't have to do anything."

But Laurie could not be passive. As his lips coaxed and his hands stroked and persuaded, she found herself wanting to touch and caress him in return. Hesitantly she reached out and put her hands around his shoulders, feeling with delight the hard bone and muscle beneath the crisp fabric of his shirt. His body trembled slightly at her touch, and he clasped her more tightly. Encouraged, she slipped her hands down from his shoulders along the line of his strong back. Her fingers seemed to have a life of their own as they explored his shoulder blades and backbone and then paused restlessly on the waistband of his slacks.

"Pull my shirt out," Craig urged her in a deep voice as he nuzzled her cheek and jaw. "Touch me, Laurie. It will feel so good to me."

Following his instructions, she tugged at the shirt and, when it was free, shyly slipped her hand beneath its hem. When she encountered Craig's naked back, she spread her fingers and ran her palm upward, glorying in the feel of his smooth, warm skin against hers.

He, too, reveled in the contact, groaning with pleasure as her fingers grew bolder. "I need to touch you, too, Laurie," he whispered. As he spoke, he maneuvered the zipper on her kaftan downward so that it fell open, revealing the creamy skin of her shoulders and the scalloped, lacy edges of her ecru bra.

For a moment Craig looked down at her, his eyes dark and unfathomable in the shadowy light. As his admiring gaze dwelt on her half-exposed breasts, Laurie felt them throb and stiffen in a way that left her breathless. When his fingers went to the front closure and unhooked it, she was incapable of protest. Brushing the lacy scraps aside, Craig's head dipped.

"Laurie, you're so beautiful," he murmured as his lips sought the stiff pink buds of her breasts. "I have to kiss you here. I've been wanting to be with you like this forever."

Laurie felt as though she were being pulled in different directions. Frightened by the novelty of what was happening, part of her wanted to stop, to draw back. But that was a very small, weak part. Most of her was yearning for this sweet intimacy. When she felt Craig's tongue draw a slow, sensual path around the sensitive crown of her breast, she was lost, paralyzed by the new sensual pleasure he was creating.

"Oh, Craig," she moaned, "what are you doing to me?"

"Just loving you," he whispered, nuzzling the vee between her throbbing breasts and then caressing the remaining creamy globe as he had the first. Each stroke of his tongue and gentle tugging pressure of his lips seemed to ignite fiery thrills of pleasure that shot through Laurie's entire being. But most of them were finding their target in the sensitive core of her femininity. And when Craig unzipped the kaftan all the way and lowered his head to the quivering flesh of her rib cage and then her stomach, those fiery darts embedded themselves more deeply, flaring to a feverish pitch.

Unconsciously she twined her fingers in Craig's thick hair and wriggled beneath him. He raised his head and gazed deeply into her dilated eyes and then loosened her hair so that it fell around her shoulders in a midnight curtain. "Unbutton my shirt, Laurie," he commanded, his voice slightly thickened. "I want to be close to you."

She obeyed without question. With fingers made clumsy by their eagerness, she began to undo his shirt. In a moment he had shrugged it off. As if she were mesmerized, Laurie flattened her palms against the broad, muscular surface of his chest, enraptured by the feel of the crisp hair and warm masculinity.

Craig waited for a moment while her hands explored him. Then, groaning with urgency, he rolled on top of her and clasped her all but naked body tightly to his.

But her reaction jarred them both from their sensual mood. She'd forgotten all about her injured thigh. As Craig's heavy leg came down on hers, she gasped as much with surprise as pain.

"Uh!"

Craig jerked away from her instantly, his face filled with concern. "What's wrong?"

"My leg . . ."

He sat up and looked down at the injured limb, noting the swelling. "Oh, my God! Laurie, I forgot about it!"

"So did I," she admitted in a small voice. As she spoke, she hastily tugged the kaftan around herself in a not very successful attempt to cover her breasts and inched up on the pillows, trying to gather her scattered wits. Craig was bending over her uncovered leg, and as she gazed down at the top of his head and naked shoulders, embarrassment mixed with regret filled her. Moments before, she had been lost to passion. Surely, if nothing had prevented them, she and Craig would have become lovers on the couch in her living room. Now the mood was cruelly shattered, and all that remained were confusion and distress.

"We should put ice on it right away," he was saying. As he spoke, he stood up and strode into the kitchen, not yet bothering to replace his shirt. After he had gone, Laurie pushed herself up farther on the couch and tried to put herself to rights. Notioing her lacy bra lying abandoned in the folds of her robe, she hastily grabbed it and stuck it under a pillow. But her uncovered breasts beneath the loose kaftan were a vivid reminder that minutes earlier Craig had kissed and caressed them and buried his face in their yearning softness.

The thought deepened the flush on Laurie's cheek, and needing something to do with her fluttering hands, she brushed back some long strands of silky black hair.

When Craig returned, he had a towel and ice cubes wrapped in another plastic bag. "Let's get this on right away," he urged as he knelt in front of the couch, slipped the folded towel under her leg, and began to arrange the improvised ice packs.

"Craig," Laurie said hesitantly, "about what was happening . . . I don't . . . I can't . . ."

Pausing in his ministrations, he rocked back on his heels and looked up at her. In the uncertain light Laurie found herself incapable of reading his expression. But when he spoke, his voice was deep and vibrantly reassuring. "I know. I apologize to you. I should be kicked around the block for taking advantage of your helplessness and innocence. You're not ready for this yet, are you, Laurie?"

Miserably she shook her head in agreement and handed Craig his shirt, which had been draped over the back of the couch. But as she watched him put it on, she wondered if her denial was really true. She'd certainly felt ready for his lovemaking earlier. And she ached now with frustration as she remembered the desire he'd aroused.

CHAPTER SIX

"I haven't heard from you since Saturday. How are things going with Craig Lawson?" Sandy's voice inquired over the phone.

Laurie stared at the receiver and wondered if her sister had ESP.

"He was over at my apartment Saturday night," she admitted cautiously, glancing at her open office door. Not only did she not want to discuss the details of that encounter with her sister, but she also didn't want to broadcast it around the Russel Corporation.

"All right," Sandy said, "I can tell you don't want to give me any details over the phone. I was calling to see if you'd like to have lunch. How about meeting me at Petrucci's?"

The invitation to eat at one of her favorite campus hangouts was tempting. But Laurie knew she couldn't spare the time. "Honest, I'm not trying to get out of talking to you since there's really nothing to say. But Hyohoto's new machinery is being uncrated now. Since I'm responsible for it, I have to stick around the building."

"That sounds plausible." Sandy chuckled. "However, I sense some subterfuge along with your good excuse. Maybe we can get together Thursday or Friday."

Laurie agreed to that. After putting down the receiver,

she turned toward the window for a moment, a thoughtful expression in her large dark eyes. Sandy was so good at reading her voice. It was lucky her sister couldn't see her face as well because she was at least partly right. Laurie was using the Hyohoto hardware as a good excuse for burying herself in so much work that she wouldn't have time to think about her relationship with Craig Lawson.

Saturday night she'd come perilously close to letting him make love to her. In fact, Craig, not she, had been the one to call a halt. How many men would have dealt with the situation so sensitively? Not many, she suspected. Did that mean that she'd been misjudging him? Or had he decided he wanted her and was simply waiting until the time was more opportune? That question and a lot of others had been chasing themselves around in her head for the last day and a half.

He'd been so attentive all Saturday. As she'd gotten ready for work on Monday, she'd admitted to herself that it was only because of Craig that she was able to walk with relative ease. The ice pack he'd insisted she use had probably made all the difference.

Though she'd half expected him to call and see how she was on Sunday, he hadn't. Maybe he didn't care as much as she'd begun to imagine. Or maybe he'd simply spent Sunday with some other, more cooperative woman.

The thought made her fingers tighten on the metal arms of her swivel chair. This sort of mental torture wasn't doing her any good, she told herself. She hadn't been lying to Sandy. She had a lot of work to do. So why was she wasting her time and energy on speculations that were leading nowhere?

Leaning forward, she dialed the number of the warehouse

section. "How far along are you on the Hyohoto shipment?" she asked.

"We've uncrated one of the machines, and Ted says it will be ready for you to test out in about twenty minutes. Want us to send it up?"

"Yes, that would be great. I'll take a lunch break now. If I'm not back when you get here, Suzy will sign for the machine."

It was early, only eleven thirty, she noted as she glanced at the clock on the wall by the elevator. With any luck she could get out of the cafeteria quickly and back to her office before that machine arrived.

But after she had filled her plate at the salad bar and found a table by the window, she was accosted by a smiling Buddy Parks.

"Hey, it's great to see you," he said enthusiastically, shifting his weight from one foot to the other. It was obvious to Laurie that he wanted to be invited to sit down. Although she was pressed for time, she didn't have the heart to disappoint him.

"I can't take long for lunch today because I have to get back to my office to check out some new equipment, but you're welcome to join me if you like," she said.

"Gee, thanks," he said, pulling out a chair. "Yeah, I heard you're on that special educational project. Really important stuff, I guess." He hesitated for a moment and then plunged on. "Say, speaking of stuff, would you mind taking a glance at my plate to see if I've picked the right things?"

Laurie looked over at the mound of lettuce covered by a selection that included carrots, celery, cottage cheese, chopped egg, and mushrooms. "That looks fine," she commented. "I think you've got the idea. And the egg and cheese will give you the protein you need."

Buddy looked like a puppy who'd just been thrown a Milk Bone. "Gee, I hope so," he said confidingly. "I've been thinking about all the things you said, and I'm determined to make some big changes in myself." He paused and then added with a self-conscious grin, "There are a lot of girls around here that I'd like to date. But I don't think I'm going to get up the courage to ask any of them out until I lose at least twenty pounds."

Laurie smiled at him sympathetically. She understood how he felt. Yet she was realistic enough to know that he would need to make some big changes if he hoped to attract coed beauties. It wasn't just the extra weight. It was the mismatched clothing and the hangdog air he projected.

She cleared her throat, wanting to be helpful yet not wanting to give offense. "You know, Buddy, it wasn't just losing weight that made a big difference for me. I worked on a lot of other things, too—like finding the clothes that looked best on me and doing something to develop a more positive self-image."

Putting down his diet cola, Buddy leaned forward. "Yeah," he said earnestly, "I was thinking about something like that, too. But I don't know where to start."

"You could try the local bookstore," Laurie said. "It has a whole section on self-improvement and fitness. There are even books for men on how to dress if you're interested. And you should talk to Ms. Campana. She can probably tell you about some other courses at the counseling center that would help."

By the time Laurie's own impromptu counseling session with Buddy was ended she'd given lunch much more time than she'd anticipated. The Hyohoto machine was already sitting in her office, along with a scrawled note from the warehouse manager.

Anxious to check it out, Laurie got out the Archimedes software and its instruction manual. A lot depended on the interface of these two halves of the project. Laurie couldn't help the nervous tremors that made her fingers fumble slightly as she inserted the first disk in the A drive. The initial routines seemed to go all right. Breathing a little more easily, she turned to some of the more sophisticated diagnostic exercises. The first two also checked out. But when she came to the third in the series, instead of completing the routine, the cursor began to move erratically around the screen as though she no longer had control of it. Finally, she had to reboot and try again.

Methodically she went through the drills a second time—with the same results.

Pushing back her chair, Laurie sighed. She'd like to be able to solve the problem herself, she thought, unconsciously gnawing on her lip and staring out the window. But that was probably going to be impossible. It could be a bug in the software, or something to do with the machine, or both. Given time, she might be able to uncover the problem herself. But the project was on a tight schedule. The most sensible course was to work closely with someone in Archimedes software design.

Reluctantly she reached for the phone and dialed Mr. Penwaithe's office. It took only a few words of explanation for her to be put through to the boss himself.

"That doesn't sound good," he muttered after she had explained the reason for her call.

"Do you think that one of the senior programmers could come down to my office this afternoon?" Laurie asked.

"Let me see what can be arranged."

A half hour later, when Craig Lawson strode into her

office, Laurie whirled around in her chair in front of the computer terminal.

"Your leg isn't giving you any problems?" he asked, smiling as though nothing unusual had happened between them.

"My leg is fine, thank you. But you didn't come to talk about my health. What are you doing here?" Laurie demanded.

He could see that she was piqued because he hadn't called since the scene on her couch last Saturday. And he couldn't blame her. Several times he'd picked up the phone and started to dial her number. But then he'd always put the receiver back down in its cradle.

Ever since that evening he'd been asking himself where he and Laurie were headed. It was no longer just a question of chasing after a good-looking woman. His feelings toward her had gotten very serious very quickly. And that was giving him pause. As he'd told Laurie, he valued his independence. One unfortunate foray into marriage had only reinforced that attitude. He wasn't even sure that he was suited to a lasting relationship with a woman. Yet in between fantasies of bedding Laurie, he found himself wondering what it would be like to grow old with her at his side.

Since their last meeting he'd been trying to persuade himself he was overreacting to her combination of beauty, brains, and innocent appeal. Yet, now that he was in her presence again, he knew that he had simply been fooling himself. This woman was important to him in a way that no other had been in the past.

His smile grew warmer. "I'm the cavalry Penwaithe called in," he informed her. "None of the programmers has worked on more than a piece of this. Since I've been coordinating the effort, I'm the only one who's got the whole picture."

Laurie looked down at the papers in front of her for a minute. His words were matter-of-fact. Yet she sensed a deeper intent behind them. She'd been confused and then angry with Craig because he hadn't called her. Now she was even more confused. What was going on in the man's mind anyway?

She'd been telling herself that she didn't want to work closely with him. Unfortunately what he claimed about his overall knowledge of the projects was probably true. Sighing, she pushed her chair back from the terminal and gestured for him to take her place in front of the monitor.

Perversely she got a measure of satisfaction when forty minutes later the confidence had been wiped from his expression. As he scowled at the screen, it was obvious that he was just as perplexed by the erratic cursor as she had been.

"I see what you mean," he muttered. "Right now this whole system is useless. If we can't get this problem ironed out quickly, the company will have to push back the project's release date."

They frowned at each other. Both knew that would be a disaster—for Russel's financial situation and its prestige in the education market.

"Let me go back to my office and get all the programming materials," Craig said, standing up and heading toward the door. "While I'm gone, you assemble every specification and reference manual you can on that machine. I'd like to hope we isolate the problem quickly, but I suspect it's going to be a long siege."

Unfortunately Craig's prediction turned out to be correct. For most of the next two days they worked together closely, testing out every hypothesis they could come up with. Though it was not an easy time, Laurie couldn't help being aware of how much worse it might have been if Craig were

95

not the sort of accommodating man he was. Since so much rode on ironing out this major glitch, tensions were high.

What's more, Laurie couldn't keep from remembering that Craig had never really been enthusiastic about using the Hyohoto hardware. It would have been easy for him to say, "I told you so," but he didn't. In fact, under the circumstances he was the soul of patience, ready with a joke or a hot cup of coffee when either was called for.

Often the work sessions stretched late into the evening, and Laurie was reminded of the companionship they'd shared in the old days. But now there was a marked difference that she was also aware of. Although Craig didn't try to make love to her again as he had on that night in her apartment, he looked at her in a new way, and the expression in his eyes was disturbing. Often, as he leaned over to scan a program she was studying, his hands brushed against her hair or her shoulder and lingered longer than was necessary. At those times Laurie had to force her mind to stay on the work at hand.

She couldn't bring herself to protest, yet she couldn't help responding to Craig's touch. Could he feel her tremble? she wondered. Did he take in her flushed appearance and realize how aware she was of him physically? He gave no sign, yet his attentions made it impossible to believe that he was oblivious or that his feelings didn't in some ways match hers.

On many levels he seemed to be much more sensitive to her needs. She couldn't help being affected by his attentiveness and consideration. Although solving this problem was as much her responsibility as his, Wednesday evening, Craig looked at her pale, drawn features and sent her home while he remained to run one or two more tests. Thursday evening, when he insisted on seeing her to her door, he kissed

96

her forehead lightly, and she couldn't bring herself to protest. All her instincts told her he cared about her. Yet he was practical enough to put their personal relationship on hold while they grappled with this serious problem at work together.

Laurie was beginning to think they might never find a solution. But Friday they got their big break. That afternoon her apologetic secretary stuck her head in the door.

"I'm sorry, Miss DiMaria," she said, "I know you requested all the documentation for the Hyohoto equipment, and I thought I'd given it to you. But this piece of material," she said, proffering a blue-bound manual, "must have come in while you were away, and somehow it got stuck in with some folders for another project."

Since Laurie was sitting behind the computer, Craig strode forward and accepted the folder from the secretary's hands. As he carried it to Laurie's desk, he began to flip through the pages. She watched as he stopped and concentrated on one particular section. "Listen," he asked, "didn't you tell me that the clock in this machine operates in milliseconds?"

"That's what I understood from the standard operating manual."

Craig lifted an eyebrow. "Well, this manual says it's operating in centiseconds. Do you think a translator got the two mixed up?"

For a moment they stared at each other. Then Laurie turned back toward the screen. "I don't know, but that would certainly account for the difficulties with the interface."

Craig set the handbook down. "Naturally, when we wrote the programs, we were assuming a clock that operated in milliseconds. Let's run some tests and check it out."

Indeed, after they'd tested their new hypothesis, the clock turned out to be the culprit. However, it was past quitting time before they were sure that they had the problem licked.

"Eureka!" Laurie crowed when they'd successfully rewritten a BASIC program to take the discrepancy into consideration. "We did it!" Grinning from ear to ear, she jumped up and turned to Craig, who was standing a few feet away.

"We sure did," he said, the triumphant gleam in his eyes reflecting her own enthusiasm as he took a step forward. In the next moment she found herself wrapped in his strong arms as he picked her up and swung her off her feet.

"This calls for a celebration," he declared.

Before she could answer, he had bent her back and his lips were descending to meet hers. He might have intended the kiss to be congratulatory, but when their mouths came together, what had begun as a joyous salute quickly changed its tenor.

"Laurie," he murmured, his breath mingling with hers and his arms tightening around her waist. Then his lips were taking hers in a fevered caress that spoke of the needs he'd been repressing all week.

Her response to his ardor was almost instantaneous. For she, too, had been suppressing the same desires. Being close to him for the past few days, sharing yet not sharing, had been torture. Now, as he pressed her body tightly against the muscled length of his, she felt herself melt into him. All her doubts and inhibitions seemed to dissolve like butter in a mug of heated rum.

Craig felt the strong emotion radiating from her and deepened the kiss. As his tongue invaded the welcoming sweetness of her mouth, he ran his hand along her spine, molding her body more completely to his.

So caught up was Laurie in the pleasure of this closeness

that she didn't even hear the phone when it began to ring. It was only the shift in Craig's body that penetrated her euphoria so that she finally became aware of the instrument's insistent summons.

She heard Craig swear under his breath. "Damn, who could that be at this hour?" he growled, looking at his watch as he reluctantly released her. "I'm afraid you'd better pick it up since this is your office."

Still a bit dazed, Laurie patted her hair into place as though the caller on the other end of the line would know what had been transpiring. By the time she picked up the phone her voice managed to sound businesslike.

"Yes?" she asked.

"Ah, Laurie," Mr. Penwaithe said, "I was afraid I'd missed you. When I called this afternoon, your secretary said you were busy, but that you'd stumbled on a promising lead. Does the fact that you're still there mean it came to naught?"

"Oh, no," she answered, looking up at Craig, who was silently mouthing the question "Penwaithe?"

Nodding to him, she continued. "We've got the problem licked," she said, almost choking when Craig leaned over to run his tongue lightly along the edge of her ear.

Giving him a stern look, she turned away so that she could maintain her concentration. "It all had to do with the clock," she said, beginning her explanation. For a few moments Craig let her continue with the recitation, but as she spoke, his hands rested on her waist, making her very aware of his closeness. Then they began to travel lightly up the sides of her rib cage, while at the same time he leaned forward and blew a stray tendril of hair off the back of her neck.

Steeling herself to ignore his attentions, Laurie doggedly

continued with the explanation. But when Craig's hands began playfully to slide around the undersides of her breasts, she had to bite her lip to keep from gasping.

"Is something wrong?" Penwaithe asked.

"Uh-uh, no!" Laurie stammered, twisting her head around and giving Craig a fierce look which made it clear that the negative was as much for him as for their boss.

"It's late, and I realize you must be tired," he was saying. "But since so much is riding on this project, I did want to get an idea of how long it would actually take to get the system functioning."

His request gave Laurie an inspiration. Smiling sweetly up into her tormentor's laughing features, she said, "Well, Craig Lawson is right here. Since he's in charge of the software end of this, I think he can give you a better account than I." Still smiling, she handed over the phone.

Craig pressed his palm against the mouthpiece. "What does he want?"

Laurie shrugged. "Oh, I don't know. He just wants to talk about the interface." As she spoke, she reached out and slipped her hand inside his suit jacket and began gently to caress the plane of his chest.

Craig sucked in his breath and then, a wicked look in his eyes, began an amazingly calm and dispassionate-sounding conversation with Mr. Penwaithe.

For a moment Laurie looked at him with admiration. Then her expression changed. Determined to disturb him as much as he had disturbed her, she moved closer and slipped open one of the buttons on his shirt. Under ordinary circumstances she would never have been so bold. But exasperation with his teasing and the euphoria of their success had made her reckless. In the next moment she had slid her warm hand inside and begun to twine the chest hair she found there around her fingers.

Although Craig continued to speak in a perfectly rational manner, his voice had taken on a husky quality. Could Mr. Penwaithe hear the change? Laurie wondered, flattening her hand against Craig's chest and moving it slowly back and forth.

He looked down, his eyes meeting hers. The smoldering fire in their green depths told Laurie just how far she had gone in this retaliatory game. She saw Craig glance meaningfully at the hand she had inserted in his shirtfront. Then, very deliberately, he reached out to touch the front of her blouse. For a heartbeat his fingers remained absolutely still. Then they began to stroke across the front of her blouse, moving from one swelling breast to the other with sensual assurance.

Laurie fought to repress a little gasp as she felt her nipples harden, closing her eyes as his knowing fingers encouraged her arousal through the thin fabric of her blouse and lacy bra.

She had almost forgotten about the phone call when she heard Craig begin to speak again. "Listen, Martin, it's been a long day. I promise to have a full report on your desk by lunchtime Monday."

The conversation went on for only a few moments longer before she heard the receiver replaced in its cradle.

"Now, where were we?" Craig asked huskily, hauling her across the few inches of space that separated them. Although he had been the one to start the sensual teasing while Laurie was on the phone, she had certainly outsmarted herself by finishing the job.

"Craig, please," she said.

He was no longer in the mood for conversation. His

101

mouth swooped to claim hers in a kiss that let her know how much her attentions had inflamed him. The teasing was over for the evening. This man wanted her—very badly.

And if the truth be known, she wanted him, too. There was no hiding from that burning certainty now, she realized as her lips parted in answer to the urgency of his kiss. She wanted so much to savor the warmth of his breath as it mingled with hers, the firmness of his lips, the caress of his tongue against the hardness of her teeth.

Then, with a deep, aching response that she was powerless to suppress, she moved her own lips and tongue against his mouth in the ways that he had taught her, instinctively seeking to give this man pleasure as well as receive it from him.

This time it was Craig who called out her name. "Ah, Laurie," he groaned. "So wonderful. So sweet."

One hand moved restlessly up and down her spine. The other cupped her bottom and pressed her lower body more closely against his, leaving no doubt that he was erect and throbbing with need for her.

There was no uncertainty in Laurie's mind about where they were headed. Though she now desperately wanted to follow where Craig was leading, she couldn't repress a stab of panic. Things were moving so quickly, yet she was such a complete novice at this sort of encounter. Except for the few times with Craig, she had hardly even kissed a man. Now they were on the brink of making love. Were they going to end up doing it right here in her office? she wondered, feeling a bubble of panic rise in her chest. What an unlikely setting she had picked for her sexual initiation.

The feeling of alarm was so strong that before Laurie realized what was happening, she had voiced her fears aloud. "This is no place to make love for the first time," she heard herself blurt and then felt her face go crimson with mortification.

Craig, who had been nuzzling his lips against the soft flesh of her neck, raised his head and looked searchingly into her face. "What did you say?" he whispered.

"I . . ." She didn't want to repeat the embarrassing utterance. Instead of finishing the sentence, she simply let herself become absorbed with a spot in the air somewhere over his left shoulder.

"Never mind, I believe I heard you."

Deliberately he released her and took a step backward, studying the suddenly tense set of her shoulders. Reaching for her hand, he led her toward the small sofa against the wall. "Let's sit down for a minute," he said.

When she had complied, he pulled over the desk chair and sat facing her. "Laurie, you said, 'This is no place to make love for the first time,' didn't you?" he asked.

Looking down at her folded hands, she nodded.

Craig reached over and gently tipped her chin up so that she was forced to meet his penetrating gaze. "Let's start with the last part first," he said softly. "Were you referring to *us*"—he hesitated for a moment—"or to yourself?"

"Both," she managed to say in a barely audible whisper.

Craig considered her answer thoughtfully. "And the first part of the sentence. Did that mean you assumed we were going to . . ." This time it was his voice that trailed off.

Unable to trust herself to speak, Laurie only nodded.

Craig leaned forward, his gaze locked with hers. "And was that what you wanted to happen?"

She had come too far with this man to be less than honest now. "Yes," she forced herself to admit.

"Laurie," he murmured, pulling her off the couch and into his lap. For a long moment he simply held her, gently

103

stroking her shoulder and neck. "Sweet Laurie." He repeated the endearment he had used in the heat of passion.

She nestled against him, enjoying the undemanding closeness, feeling infinitely warm and safe in his arms. She knew he was giving her time to think things through, to reconsider her declaration in a cooler frame of mind. He wouldn't force the issue. She knew that now. He was leaving the rest of the evening up to her. Yet, although she had made her decision, she didn't quite know how to voice it.

"Craig," she finally said, drawing back slightly so that she could look into his eyes, "I was wondering if you'd like to give me a ride home and then stay for dinner."

He smiled warmly at her, reaching out to trace the outline of her lips with his thumb. "Actually I think I've imposed on your hospitality enough," he said. "Why don't we go back to my place—if that's all right with you?"

"Yes. Fine." She agreed quickly. "I've been wanting to see where you lived."

"And I've been wanting to show you."

CHAPTER SEVEN

Quickly they left the all but empty building and headed for the parking lot. After Craig had helped Laurie into his car and slid behind the wheel, he shot her a quick glance. She was sitting with her head angled slightly away, her hands interlaced in her lap.

For a moment he studied her profile before reaching over to squeeze her fingers reassuringly. He was remembering the way she'd been embarrassed by the love scenes in the movie they'd seen together, the way she had kissed him afterward in the kitchen, and the way she had reacted in panic when he'd started to undo her dress. He had been almost sure for a long time that she was a virgin.

Yet even with all the evidence he hadn't been prepared for her blurted admission back there in the office. It had both surprised and touched him. Now once again he felt tender emotions toward her welling up inside him. He'd known for a long time that Laurie wasn't just another beautiful woman he wanted to take to bed. His feelings for her were much stronger than that, and he had to believe that her feelings for him were also more than superficial—or why would she be on her way to his house now? Back at the office he had given her an opportunity to change her mind. She hadn't taken him up on the offer. That had to mean something.

Nevertheless, as he swung out of the parking space, Craig could see that Laurie was far from relaxed. He watched as her teeth worried her bottom lip and her fingers curled and uncurled in her lap. But, then, what did he expect? he asked himself. This was something new for her and therefore almost certainly frightening.

After a few moments of silence Craig reached over and turned on the radio. At least they both could pretend to be listening to the music, he thought.

"We're almost there," he finally informed her.

"Oh." The neighborhood, Laurie noticed, was a lot like Sandy's. Sure enough, they drew up in front of a large Victorian house with wide porches on three sides and a splendid turret at the fourth.

But while the general appearance was similar to her sister's, the interior was quite different. Craig's furnishings were for the most part modern. He had used them as a foil to set off the fine antique oak floors, mantelpieces, and brass fixtures of his house, all of which had been lovingly restored to their original splendor.

Glad to take her mind off her nervous fears about what the evening held, Laurie looked around with real interest. "All this work must have cost a fortune," she finally ventured to say.

"It would have," Craig commented, "except that I did most of the work myself. I didn't even know how to use a power sander when I first spotted the For Sale sign on this place and fell in love with it. But I knew that if I were going to realize the house's potential and not pump all my salary into workmen's fees, I'd have to learn some handyman skills."

Laurie nodded, looking at him with new respect. He'd gone a lot beyond the mere handyman stage.

"Come on into the kitchen," Craig said. "I'm going to put you to work chopping vegetables."

As she followed him down the hall, Laurie's mind was racing. How well did she really know Craig Lawson? she wondered. Had she really told him she was coming here to make love? It was one thing to allow herself to be swept off her feet in the heat of passion and quite another deliberately to come to his house and proclaim herself ready to jump into bed. What would he say if she announced that she had changed her mind after all?

The disturbing thought made Laurie feel trapped. And it didn't help when Craig took off his jacket and rolled up his shirt-sleeves. Even when he was preparing to cook dinner, she couldn't help noticing the way he radiated a sort of elemental masculinity. As he reached for the soy sauce, she could see the play of muscles in his arm. Suddenly she was vividly reminded of how strong—and assertive—he could be when he wanted something.

"I hope you like fresh ginger," he was saying, "because that's the secret ingredient in this marinade."

Laurie nodded tightly and then pretended to inspect the kitchen. Like Sandy's, it was splendid, with fine old cabinetry. But Craig had also left the original cast-iron stove sitting across the room from his modern bank of appliances.

"You're not going to cook on that?" Laurie asked, pointing to the formidable black monstrosity.

Craig set down a box of brown sugar and grinned. "I don't usually. But it is in working order, and it *has* come in handy when the power's gone off."

"I guess I'd be afraid it would blow up or something," Laurie observed dryly.

Craig could tell from the tone of her voice that she was feeling uncomfortable. He gave her a direct look over his shoulder. "Listen, Laurie, I did promise you dinner. If you want to leave after you've eaten, I'll drive you home."

"I didn't mean . . ." She started to protest, well aware that he knew very well what she meant.

But he shook his head. "It's all right. I understand. Besides, I thought I made it perfectly clear that I'm not out to force myself on you."

Laurie looked down at the toes of her leather pumps so that he couldn't see the flush spreading across her features. "Craig, I'm sorry," she mumbled.

"You don't have anything to be sorry about. But you will if you don't help me cut up the vegetables for my stir-fry. I was counting on a kitchen assistant, you know."

Thank goodness he was making this easy for her, Laurie thought. "What do you want me to cut?" she asked lightly, as though he really had just asked her over for a simple dinner between friends and as though they were not a man and a woman who had talked about becoming lovers less than a half hour before.

As they worked, Craig asked friendly questions about her Oriental cooking skills. It wasn't long before she was feeling much more at ease in his presence.

"Sit down, and I'll be right back," Craig told her after they had carried the serving dishes to the chrome and glass dining-room table. As she pulled out her chair, Laurie heard the refrigerator door open. A moment later Craig reappeared with a bottle of fine French champagne and two long-stemmed glasses.

"I told myself we were going to solve that problem with the Archimedes project," he announced, beginning to untwist the wires at the top of the bottle, "and as a sort of portent of success, I got this to celebrate."

As they toasted the project, Laurie studied Craig's face.

There were circles under his eyes that she hadn't noticed before. Was it her imagination, or were there faint lines of tension around his mouth? She hadn't stopped to think that this crisis might have been taking its toll on him or that his feelings during the ordeal might have been similar to hers.

She had been so wrapped up in her own doubts that she hadn't thought to ask about his. Instead of sharing his worries, he had worked hard to give her the support she needed. The insight gave her a lot to think about, and for a few moments they ate without speaking.

"Well, I hope you're silent because you like my ginger chicken," Craig finally said.

Laurie looked across the table and smiled. "It's delicious. The best meal I've had all week," she replied sincerely.

He seemed quite pleased. "I was hoping you'd like it. Actually it wasn't just the champagne that I bought with you in mind. One evening to keep myself from worrying about the project, I went grocery shopping and got this stuff."

"I know what you mean," Laurie said. "A few days ago I went to the library and got out a bunch of Stephen King books that I'd been wanting to read. You don't know how much easier it was worrying about mad dogs and haunted hotels in the evenings than the stuff I had left behind at work."

Craig threw back his head and laughed. "Well, that's one way to cope," he said.

The conversation went on easily from there as they enjoyed their food and wine together. Laurie couldn't help marveling again at how much she really did enjoy Craig's company.

After he had finished his second helping of chicken and rice, Craig pushed his chair slightly away from the table and leaned back comfortably. For a moment he studied Laurie's face and then grinned a bit self-consciously.

"Don't laugh, but you know, there's one more reward I kept hoping to treat myself to," he said. "I kept thinking about how I'd like to take you out dancing."

"Dancing?" Laurie responded. "Why dancing?"

Craig shrugged. "I'm not sure. But you know how your mind gets in a particular groove and stays there."

Laurie nodded. She had done that kind of thing herself— but not with regard to dancing. Actually she'd never considered herself much of a dancer. If her mother hadn't insisted on lessons when she was in junior high school, she probably wouldn't know how.

"Craig, you're likely to be disappointed in me as a partner," she said aloud.

He smiled. "I doubt it. But we can find out easily enough. Let me clear the table, and then I'll put some music on the stereo."

Laurie was about to demur when she caught the look of boyish enthusiasm in Craig's face. He really did want to dance with her. And why not? After all, he hadn't asked for anything in return while he'd kept up her spirits.

"All right," she said. "But let me help you put the plates into the dishwasher first."

The cleanup chores were accomplished quickly. Craig dimmed the lights in the living room before putting a stack of records on the automatic changer.

"Come on," he said invitingly, holding out a hand.

"Remember, I told you I'm not very good," Laurie said in protest.

Craig ignored the disclaimer and pulled her into his arms. "All you have to do is relax and let me lead you," he told her.

It took only a few moments to realize that he was right. He was easy to follow.

"You must have been putting me on. You're good at this," he whispered, his breath warm against her ear.

The contact made Laurie shiver slightly in his arms. She had been so eager to accommodate his whim that she hadn't stopped to think that it would mean getting so near to him again. Or maybe she had been subconsciously hoping for an excuse to do just that.

Almost as though he wanted to test the point, Craig drew his left arm more tightly around her so that the length of her body was brought into closer contact with his. As he had hoped, Laurie made no protest.

For a little while, as they swayed to the romantic music, Craig was content. But soon his hand began to move across her back and shoulders and then upward so that his fingers could twine with the wisps of dark hair that had come loose from her French twist.

Laurie sighed and closed her eyes. She felt enveloped by the warmth and strength of his supple body. It was impossible to keep the hand that rested against his back from stroking a small circle of its own against the fabric of his shirt.

"That feels so good," Craig murmured. "Don't stop."

Obediently Laurie widened the circle, enjoying the contact with his firm muscles and the strong frame beneath. Raising her head, she looked up at him, her dark eyes large and luminous. For a moment his gaze caressed her features before he lowered his face toward hers.

She could feel the curve of a welcoming smile on his lips as they found hers. He tasted of champagne and ginger, and her mouth opened automatically under his. Which of them deepened the kiss? She didn't know or care. For at the barest touch of his lips against hers, she realized how hungry she was for the taste of Craig Lawson. It was the same fiery hunger that had been kindled back in her office. And though the flame had been banked by her nervous doubts and second thoughts, it had not gone out. Instead, it had been waiting patiently within her for the right moment to flare to life again.

She felt his tongue sink deep into the warm cavity of her mouth, the gesture so totally possessive that there could be no doubt that he shared the intensity of her hunger. Yet in the next instant he had torn his lips away from hers and shifted his body so that he could put a few inches of distance between them.

"Laurie." His voice was thick and unsteady as he fought to control the aching need she had evoked. "I said I'd take you home. If you want to leave, it had better be right now."

For a moment she was silent as she studied the intensity of his face. She could leave now. Craig would take her home; she had no doubt of that.

But was that what she really wanted? Craig had been the focus of her yearnings for so long. So much of her energy had gone into resisting him that it had become a habit. Yet over the past several weeks he'd shown her a side of himself that she suspected few women had seen. All her instincts told her that this was a chance to change things between them—a chance she shouldn't pass up.

"I'd like to stay here with you," she finally said, her voice as emotion-charged as his had been. She didn't know that the fires he had ignited danced in her eyes now—as much an invitation as her words.

"Laurie," he repeated on a sigh of relief, pulling her close against him once more. If she had wanted to leave him now, it would have been like having his heart cut out with a blunt knife. His hands caressed her back and shoulders again before traveling downward to trace the lines of her hips and derriere with a more assertive possessiveness.

She wanted to touch him, too, to experience this wondrous evening with him to the fullest possible extent. The time for maidenly modesty was long past, she told herself, tugging at the back of his shirt so that she could free it from his waistband. Sighing, she slipped her hands underneath, rubbing them sensuously against the warmth of his skin.

Craig drew back slightly, unaware that his face was a mixture of passion and amusement. "I think if we're getting to the undressing stage, it might be time to withdraw to the bedroom," he pointed out.

Despite her bold resolve, Laurie couldn't stop a warm flush from creeping into her cheeks. "I didn't mean . . ." she said.

Craig shook his head. Before she could finish the sentence, he reached out to press a finger against her lips and then traced their delicate pink outline. Unwilling to break the contact, he went on to caress their inner surface and the serrated line of her white teeth beyond. Laurie found his fingertip with her tongue.

"Actually I was going to make the suggestion anyway," he murmured, extending his hand toward Laurie's. Without speaking they ascended the wide staircase together.

Craig's bedroom was the first room on the right. Only a small hanging lamp in the corner was lit, but Laurie could see the clean, unencumbered lines of the dark wood furnishings within. Stopping at the entrance, Craig pointed to a door at the other side of the room. "Laurie, there's a bathroom through there. I'll be back in a little while," he added.

Laurie watched him retreat down the hall, step into another room, and close the door. He was again being considerate, she knew, giving her time to get ready for him in privacy.

After a glance at the wide bed covered with a gold comforter, she crossed to the bathroom. It was decorated in tans and golds and smelled of Craig's aftershave lotion. He was taking a chance leaving her alone in here, she thought with a nervous giggle as she pulled the door shut behind her. It gave her a good opportunity for second thoughts. She bit her lip. *You're not trying to talk yourself out of this, are you?* she asked herself once again. She knew that this time the answer was no.

Despite her resolve, she still couldn't help feeling like a novice actress with stage fright. A few minutes later, as she washed her hands, she gave her face a quick inspection in the wood-framed mirror above the old-fashioned pedestal sink. Her lipstick was completely gone. Her eyes were over-bright, and her cheeks slightly flushed. With fingers that trembled, she began to undo the now disheveled French twist that still held most of her hair in place. Shaking her head, she watched as her thick dark tresses swirled around her shoulders.

With one ear tuned to detect the sound of Craig's returning footsteps, she bent to remove her pantyhose and then began to undo the buttons of her dress. What should she wear? she wondered. Pants and bra? That seemed prudish under the circumstances. Nothing at all? What if he came back and caught her emerging from the bathroom naked? She'd probably jump back inside and pull the door shut after herself.

Craig's short terry robe hanging on the back of the door was the solution to her problem. After removing the rest of her clothing as rapidly as possible, she slipped on the tan wrapper. Her hand hesitated on the knob for an instant before she opened the door.

Grateful that Craig had not yet returned, she dashed across the room and turned down the gold coverlet. Then, with a furtive glance at the door, she undid the robe and flung it off. After tossing it to the foot of the bed, she slipped quickly between the sheets, pulling the covers modestly up over the tops of her breasts.

Maybe Craig had been waiting for her return to the bedroom, she decided. In a few moments he reappeared, still wearing his slacks and white shirt.

He paused in the doorway, his eyes warm and ardent while he took in her presence in his bed. His breath caught in his chest as his gaze traveled over her raven tresses spread across the pillow and the rich olive of her skin against the pale sheets. He could see no lower than her shoulders. Yet, since they were bare, the rest of her must be that way under the covers. How many times had he dreamed of finding her here like this? he wondered, crossing the room to seat himself on the edge of the bed. Reaching out, he found a lock of her dark hair against the pillow and wove it between his fingers.

"Lovely and silky," he murmured, bringing the strands up to his lips. She looked so vulnerable, he thought, knowing that it would break her heart—and his as well—if he were not tender and caring with her tonight. Bending over her, he pulled Laurie gently into his arms. With only a little hesitation her arms moved up from under the covers to clasp his shoulders.

His lips, warm and knowing, found hers then. The kiss began as softly as the whisper of the spring wind through the trees. But when Laurie licked playfully at the corner of his lips and then slid her tongue between his teeth, it quickly escalated to hurricane force, leaving them almost breathless.

"Ah, Laurie," he groaned deep in his chest, nuzzling his lips against her cheek, her chin, her neck. And then he was standing up so that he could remove his clothing.

"Aren't you going to turn off the light?" she whispered, unable to keep her voice entirely steady. He had already discarded his shirt. She knew she wasn't quite bold enough to watch him shed his pants.

"No. I want to see you when I make love to you, Laurie," he told her.

The words sent a shiver of anticipation through her body, as though they had been an intimate caress.

In the next moment he was naked in the bed beside her, pulling her into his arms again.

"God, Laurie, finally to hold you like this," he whispered huskily, his hands sliding greedily along the silky length of her body. There was both gratification and sensual tension in the contact.

This was something new and wonderful, she thought, burying her face in the curly hair that spread across his broad chest so that she could lose herself in the feel and the scent of his body.

"I'm glad we're here, not on that couch of yours or that ridiculous futon," she heard him growl in her ear. Raising her head, she found him grinning at her and couldn't repress an answering grin.

He reached out to smooth a wayward strand of hair back from her forehead. "I'm also glad you still have your sense of humor," he added.

"Maybe that's the only thing that's keeping me from quaking in my absent boots," she returned as lightly as possible.

At the words his face grew more serious. "Laurie, I know making love is"—he hesitated—"new for you. But I need your help if I'm going to make this as good for you as it can be."

"What do you want me to do?" she asked tremulously.

"Trust your feelings. Don't hold back. Don't be afraid of me. And don't be afraid to tell me what you like and what you don't like."

As he spoke, his hand reached out to caress her shoulders and then moved downward to glide across her breasts, stroking a random sensual path from one to the other before seeking out their hardening tips.

"Does that feel good?" he murmured.

"Oh, yes. But you must know that," she whispered.

"Yes. But I can't always know what feels best. You're going to have to tell me that."

"Craig, I don't know if I can," she said.

"It doesn't necessarily have to be with words," he answered.

Slowly then he pulled back the covers so that he could repeat the caress with his lips and tongue. Laurie made a small sound in her throat, unable to believe the flood of sensations he was creating. But it was only the beginning. With hands and lips gentle and knowing on her body, he set about to arouse her even further, seeking and learning what would give her the most pleasure.

For Laurie, there was no pulling back this time, no drawing away, even when she felt his hand on the silky skin of her inner thigh.

Reassuringly he kissed her cheek, her lips, her brows as his fingers moved upward to stroke and caress the very center of her femininity and then to slip inside her.

He bent to catch her little gasps of pleasure with his own

117

lips. He could sense her arousal reaching a peak of sensation —sense it in the fine sheen of perspiration that covered her body and in the increasing raggedness of her breathing. Though he wanted desperately to complete their union and knew that in a certain sense she would be ready for him now, he realized, too, that it would be better for her if he waited. He wanted her to know what the ultimate experience would be like first, know what feelings she was striving toward when he finally joined their bodies and began to move inside her.

It was worth waiting to assuage his own need, he told himself, to watch her face as she approached the peak of ecstasy.

"Craig," she gasped, unprepared for the very intensity of the needs and desires he was creating.

"Laurie, don't hold back now. It's all right. Just let it happen," he told her.

Again he began to caress the warm, liquid core of her desire. And this time his other hand moved to her breasts to feather a path from one hardened crest to the other.

"Craig," she gasped again, unable now to resist the shock waves of pleasure that washed over her. Convulsively her hands gripped his shoulders, as though she were trying to keep from being swept away by a storm of unfamiliar sensations. He watched the tremors subside and then pulled her into his arms and pressed his lips against the damply glistening skin where her neck and shoulder met.

Drawing back slightly, he smiled down into her still passion-drugged eyes.

"God, you're so damn sexy," he whispered huskily.

"Am I?" The question held a note of disbelief, as much in what had just happened to her as in his words.

"Yes. Very damn sexy." For a few moments he simply

held her, and then it was impossible to contain himself. His lips and hands began to seek her again. When he felt her respond more quickly this time, he couldn't resist a chuckle as his teeth nipped playfully at the lobe of her ear. "Very damn sexy," he repeated.

More sure of herself now, Laurie began to caress his body as well, seeking to give back a measure of what she had received from him.

"Laurie, I like that too damn much." His voice sounded hoarse even to his own ears. "If you keep that up, I won't be able to wait."

Her arms went around his shoulders to pull him close. "You told me to tell you what I wanted," she whispered against his neck. "Well, I want you inside me now."

He drew back to look down into the dark pools of her eyes, seeing his need mirrored there.

"What do you want me to do?" she asked.

Despite the directness of the words, he felt her tremble slightly. Gently he parted her legs with one of his own so that he could lie between them. Even though he knew how much she wanted this, he felt the tension in her body increase.

"Not yet. Not until you're ready," he murmured. For a long moment he simply held her, letting her adjust to his weight. Then he began to rock gently against her with slow, seductive sensuality. He wanted to sink into her, to let her warmth envelop him. But somehow he forced himself to hold back until he felt her body begin to move with his and knew she was succumbing to the sensations he was creating.

"Laurie, tilt your hips up for me," he told her.

She did as he asked and then felt him poised against her. Again he forced himself to go slowly, watching her face closely. He saw her jaw clench and heard her little gasp of pain when it was too late for him to stop. But that part of it was over almost as quickly as it had begun.

As he began to move inside her, he felt her arms tighten around his waist. And he heard the passion in her voice as she called his name over and over.

She had thought that he had taken her to the heights of sensation before. But it was nothing compared to what it was like having him inside her now. She felt the tempo of their rapture increase, driving her to plateaus of sensation she hadn't known existed. And when her shattering release came this time, she knew that he was right there with her, sharing the ecstasy.

Pulling Laurie against his side, Craig cradled her in his arms and felt her snuggled against his warmth. Now that the heat of their passion had been spent, the room felt chilly. Reaching down, he pulled the covers over them again.

"How are you?" he asked. As he spoke, his lips traced a line from her temple to the corner of her mouth.

"Can't you tell?"

"I mean, besides damn sexy," he said teasingly.

"Craig!"

She heard laughter rumble deep in his chest. "I'm sure I could provide another demonstration tonight. But don't tempt me. It's been quite a day for you, and I think you need your rest."

"Mmmm," she said in agreement, snuggling closer against him, feeling more totally drained yet at the same time more totally fulfilled than she ever had before in her life.

CHAPTER EIGHT

Hesitantly, in slow stages, Laurie swam upward through layers of fog. She wasn't entirely sure she wanted to surface from sleep. Though only barely conscious, somehow she knew this was an unusual morning.

Keeping her eyes firmly shut, she moved her arm, and her fingers spread to take in the cushiony feel of the mattress and smooth texture of the sheet beneath her. She wasn't lying on her futon. But there was something else strange: a clean, masculine aroma and a warmth just beyond her hand. Automatically she reached toward it, and then her seeking fingers froze. She was touching skin. And it wasn't on her body.

Still, afraid of what she might see, she didn't open her eyes. Her mind scurried like a caged squirrel. What had happened last night? Where was she? Pictures that left her breathless began to form in her mind, and at that moment all her confused doubts were scattered to the winds when a large, warm hand wrapped itself around hers and squeezed gently.

Her dark eyes flew open, and she found herself staring directly at a mat of curling black chest hair. It adorned the upper half of a very muscular and quite naked male torso and then continued downward. For an instant her gaze dipped lower to note with relief that the narrow hips opposite hers were covered by a sheet. But the material had slipped suggestively so that it just barely swathed the swell of a firm masculine buttock and revealed the hair-sprinkled indentation that dimpled the flat surface of a hard male belly.

The sight made her gaze skitter frantically to her own unclothed self. The hem of the same truant sheet rested on her waist, too. Above it her upper regions were bare, her naked breasts exposed. Convulsively she dragged her fingers away from the hand that had captured them in order to jerk the sheet upward. But her action was interrupted by an explosion of baritone laughter.

"It's a little late now for maidenly modesty, don't you think? I've been lying awake here for half an hour admiring your breasts."

Finally, at the sound of Craig's voice, Laurie looked up and met his eyes. And as she encountered their sparkling green depths, she remembered with piercing clarity everything that had happened the night before. She was no longer Laurie DiMaria, the trembling, inexperienced virgin. She had been made love to—passionately and expertly. In one incredibly fulfilling night everything had been changed. She was in Craig Lawson's house, lying naked in his bed, and the man she had dreamed about for years was now her very real lover. She was too stunned by the realization to be quite sure of her reaction. And Craig didn't give her time to think about it.

Reaching out, he gently tugged the sheet from her fingers and pushed it back down the silky length of her slender body so that it once again draped only the seductive swell of her hips.

"And beautiful breasts they are," he murmured huskily,

his gaze seeming to feast on the quivering mounds with their rosy tips that stiffened under his scrutiny.

"You've been lying there watching me sleep all this time?" she inquired breathlessly.

Warm glints flickered in Craig's green eyes as he lifted them to her face. "Yes."

"But why?"

"Because you're so beautiful, and when you're asleep, lying in my bed so sweet and vulnerable, you're especially beautiful." His voice deepened. "But now that you're awake, you're more beautiful than ever, and I want to do more than just look."

Laurie gazed at him from under lowered lashes, conscious of the change in his attitude toward her. Last night he had been introducing her into the mysteries of sensual love and had treated her like an initiate. This morning he was treating her like his woman.

As he spoke, he bent his head and kissed the rosy tip of each pulsing globe. "I've been wanting to do that ever since I saw you lying next to me." He lifted his head and smiled up at her again. "When I opened my eyes this morning, I thought I was still dreaming. I had to touch your hair to make sure I wasn't imagining things. And then I just lay here and looked at you until you woke up." Having taken a dark velvet strand between his fingers, he touched his lips to it. "God, Laurie, with your hair spread like black silk around your shoulders and your skin so smooth and satiny, it was like coming to consciousness in paradise and finding myself in bed with a houri."

Laurie was both flattered and bemused by the idea. "A houri?"

"Mmmm . . ." Craig grinned wickedly as he went on to explain. "Houris . . . beautiful black-eyed nymphs who dwell in the Mohammedan heaven. I can understand now why the Moslems conquered so much territory and why the fierce warriors of that faith were so willing to die and go to their heavenly reward," he said jokingly, as his gaze began another scorching tour of her body.

The intimacy of his inspection made Laurie blush, but at the same time tingles of pleasure spread through her body. No one had ever before talked to her like this. She'd never experienced a lover's possessive gaze on her nakedness as she was doing now, and suddenly she knew how Eve must have reacted in the garden when Adam first really saw her. The feeling was as old and as primitive as time and as new and fresh as the moment. It made her piercingly conscious that she was a woman, a woman who could please her man —and who wanted to please her man.

Slowly Craig's hands reached out and spanned the narrow width of her waist. "You're so small and lovely," he murmured huskily. "Every inch of you is lovely."

Leaning down, he kissed the soft skin of her rib cage above his hands. Then his lips moved upward until they were once more on her breasts, nibbling sensually and bathing them in the sweet dew of his mouth. The delicate, feathery movements on her sensitized flesh had their effect. Her breasts throbbed and yearned with excitement. Her skin began to flush, and her hands went to his shoulders, where they kneaded his skin convulsively.

"Oh, Craig," she whispered, all her doubts vanishing as she arched her back and abandoned herself to the pleasure he was creating.

"Oh, Laurie," he answered in a thickened voice. "I can't resist you."

Moving up, he pressed his length to her, and when their hips met, she felt the truth of what he'd said. His manhood, cradled suggestively in the valley between her legs, was fully aroused.

"You see how you affect me," he asked in a tone that was almost accusing.

"Yes," she admitted just before his mouth came down to silence her and his urgent body pressed her yielding softness into the mattress. Than all rational thought vanished as she was swept away in a torrent of heady, mesmerizing feelings.

It was much later that morning before Laurie left Craig's bed. And then, at his insistence, her trip was a short one—only a few feet away to take a shower with him. Another first, she thought as she looked down at his damp hair. She'd given him a shampoo, taking delight in rubbing the fragrant soap into his thick hair and running her fingers through the wet strands. Now he was insisting on doing the same for her. Only the area he wished to shampoo was not located on top of her head. He was kneeling before her in the shower stall, planting kisses on her hips and stomach while he soaped and washed the dark triangle at the top of her thighs.

Never in her wildest dreams had she imagined herself being tended adoringly in a shower stall by Craig Lawson, and she was finding the experience a bit unnerving. "Craig," she said protestingly, tugging playfully at his curls, "stop it. I'm so clean now you could eat dinner on me."

He shot her a wicked look that made her redden and then giggle. "Now that's an idea that appeals. I could start with a white wine in a perfect goblet," he said musingly, dipping his tongue into the pearl of clean moisture caught by the shallow dimple of her navel. "And I won't have any trouble finding an appetizer." He ran his hands suggestively down the lissome line of her naked body, pausing to caress her breasts, stomach, and thighs. "There certainly are a lot of appetizing things on this banquet table," he growled. "And it all looks absolutely delicious."

Laurie didn't know how to respond. She was being treated to a kind of love play that was totally unfamiliar to her. What did it mean? Were any of these compliments sincere? Or did Craig say these things to all his women? This last thought was so painful that she quickly pushed it away. Better to enjoy this wondrous new experience and not ruin it by asking too many questions, she warned herself.

But her doubts refused to be kept in abeyance long, and the same questions were again running through Laurie's mind when Craig, whistling cheerfully, went down to fix their breakfast and left her alone in his bedroom to dress. What had last night meant to him? What did he really feel about her? It had been an incredible and unique experience for her. But for him?

As she bent down to pick up her underwear, she glanced at herself in the mirror and paused. For a long time after her weight loss, she'd been disoriented about her personal appearance. Having thought of herself as fat and frumpy for so long, she'd simply not been able to get used to the sleek, fashionably dressed woman she'd become. Indeed, it often happened that she would catch glimpses of her reflection as she walked down a city street or paused in front of a store to admire a window display, and she would not recognize the attractive image in the mirrors as herself.

Just for a split second that happened in Craig's room now. When she looked up and saw the delicately made dark-haired nymph reflected above his bureau, she wondered who it was. Straightening, she moved toward the mirror and studied what it held. Her smooth olive skin was still damp from the shower and ruddy from the attentions of a thorough and persistent lover.

It covered an undeniably pretty oval face and a body that was sleek and perfect. Her thick hair hung in a velvety sweep of midnight around her shoulders, and there was something knowing in the uptilted dark eyes that hadn't been there before.

The reflection showed a woman who displayed all of nature's finest feminine gifts—one, though Laurie didn't say as much to herself, whom almost any man would be attracted to and who would not lack for anything she reasonably desired. To Laurie, the beautiful creature there was familiar and at the same time totally alien. She had spent so much time lacking the things this vision of loveliness could claim so easily that it was difficult to associate herself with her almost brand-new alter ego. But the woman reflected was the one who had received the loving of Craig's body last night and again this morning. This slim, perfect brunette was the woman he'd pursued and finally had gotten into his bed. It must be this woman he wanted—if only for a little while.

And she's me, Laurie told herself, turning away from the inexplicably disturbing mirror and quickly tugging on her clothes.

When she was dressed, she made the bed and then went downstairs. In the hallway the fragrance of fresh coffee greeted her. When she entered the kitchen, other equally tempting aromas assaulted her nostrils.

"You're doing so much cooking for me I'm beginning to feel guilty," she said in protest, taking note of the creamy omelets and cinnamon toast Craig was producing on top of his stove.

"I like cooking for you, but if you mean that about feeling guilty, you can fix my meal tonight," he retorted, shooting her a welcoming grin as he took the coffeepot off the burner and poured her a mugful.

As she accepted the cup, her eyes drank him in. Freshly showered and shaved and wearing a navy polo shirt along with jeans that fitted his trim hips snugly, he was the picture of casually virile good looks—the perfect complement to the female image she'd seen in the mirror upstairs. Again the thought gave her a twinge of discomfort, and determined not to let anything spoil her morning with Craig, she pushed it aside.

"May I help?" she asked brightly.

Craig shook his head. "The table's already set. Nothing for you to do now but sit down and look beautiful while I serve your eggs and toast."

Unaccountably Laurie felt another slight stab of irritation at the statement. He had spoken to her as though she were a useless doll who could do nothing but sit around looking pretty. But that was an irrational reaction, she admitted to herself, and the thought vanished as he came toward her, carrying a platter loaded with the breakfast he'd prepared. It smelled delicious, and as she took an appreciative sip of her coffee, she realized just how hungry she was. This wasn't really breakfast, after all, but more like brunch since they'd spent so much time in bed that it was now almost noon. The realization made her gaze dart to Craig's face. But he was too busy filling her dish to take note.

"What do you want to do after we eat?" he was asking casually.

Laurie took another sip of her coffee. "Well, I suppose I should go home. I'm not really comfortable in these clothes now," she added, looking down at the tailored dress and pumps she'd worn to work yesterday.

"It would be okay with me if you left them off altogether," Craig said teasingly as he handed her a glass of golden juice. "But I know what you mean. Saturday is for jeans. How about my taking you back to your place so you can change and grab whatever you need to spend the rest of the weekend here?"

Laurie chewed her eggs without tasting them, her mind whirling. Last night she'd made a big decision. Now Craig was asking her to make another. It was one thing to spend the night with him. But it seemed like something quite different to commit herself to an entire weekend.

"What will we do?" she asked, her fork poised over her plate as she waited for his reply.

Craig's emerald eyes caressed her face. "Anything you like—take walks, read books, talk. Of course, there's no doubt in my mind about what I really want to spend most of the time doing. But that will depend on you, Laurie."

Her gaze dropped away from his. She didn't quite know how to respond. Of course, she wanted to make love with him again. At the thought her whole body throbbed with anticipatory excitement. Craig had introduced her to a world of sensual pleasure she'd never really known existed. It was inevitable that she would desire to taste that pleasure again in his arms. But it was one thing to think these thoughts and another to say them out loud.

"We can go after we've finished our coffee," she murmured.

Craig reached across the table and caressed the soft palm of her hand. "Good girl!"

When they arrived at her apartment a little later in the day, Laurie quickly changed into jeans and a blue and white striped cotton blouse. It took only minutes for her to throw a few necessities into a tote bag, and when that was done, they left and traveled down to the lobby in a pleasantly deserted elevator. As they pulled out of the parking lot, she glanced back, secretly relieved they hadn't run into Art Frazier. Since she'd met him that first day, he'd made several attempts to date her, and it would have been embarrassing to run into him again when she was with Craig.

"What now?" Laurie inquired as Craig pulled out of his space and headed back toward his side of town.

He grinned at her. "Just as I said before, anything you like. What's your pleasure, milady?"

Laurie looked around. It was a fine day. The sky was an unclouded blue, and the air was clear and warm. Though the trees and bushes had exchanged their first tender green for fully developed leaves of a darker hue, there was still a freshly minted quality about them. And she herself felt freshly minted—a new Laurie, who had embarked on a new adventure.

"How about taking a picnic to the arboretum?" she suggested. "I'll fix it since you prepared dinner and breakfast."

"Great! I'll stop at a grocery store so we can pick up everything we need." He shot her a wicked leer. "The arboretum's a wonderful place. It's almost always deserted, and I know some very private spots there where we won't be disturbed."

It turned out that Craig hadn't been exaggerating his expert knowledge of the natural, hilly area that overlooked the university's campus. After he and Laurie had spent most of the afternoon walking the trails and admiring the fine weather and spectacular plantings, he led her to a knoll with a spectacular view that was screened by a thick stand of bushes and the trailing fronds of a crown of weeping willows.

"This is where we should have our picnic," he said, gesturing at the wild flower-sprinkled carpet of grass at their feet.

Laurie couldn't keep from eyeing him suspiciously. "You came to this secluded little den through all that wilderness as surefootedly as though you were an Indian guide. You obviously know this place. Have you been here often before?"

"Yes," Craig admitted, spreading their blanket flat and tugging her down next to him. "But never with a lady as lovely as you."

He was slightly annoyed at her question. She knew that he'd dated other women. But what did that matter? This was a favorite spot of his, and he'd wanted to share it with Laurie. From now on the only memories it harbored would be of her.

She seemed to accept his simple statement, looking around and admiring the view. But there was a slight pucker on her normally smooth forehead that he didn't like. Reaching out, he smoothed it with his fingers and then touched his lips to it. "I've been wanting to get my hands on you all afternoon," he said lightly. But under the teasing surface there was a serious note that acted on Laurie like an aphrodisiac. She'd been wanting his hands on her all afternoon, too. All the while they'd explored the deserted trails together and exclaimed over the scenery, she'd been thinking of the moment he would take her in his arms again and make love to her.

"Last night and this morning were wonderful, Laurie, but they weren't enough."

She looked at him mutely, too confused by her jumbled feelings to be able to articulate them.

But Craig wasn't looking for an answer in words. He slid

his mouth down the olive skin of her throat, pausing to graze on the warm, pulsing area behind her ear.

"So far this has been a wonderful day," he whispered. "Let's make it even more wonderful."

When his lips found hers, he sensed a fleeting resistance. But it melted as he deepened the kiss and stroked his hands down her back and sides. And it disappeared altogether when his lips found the beating hollow of her throat and then slid to the vee between her breasts as he slowly unbuttoned her blouse.

"Oh, Craig, someone might—"

"No, we haven't seen a soul all day, and this spot is practically invisible," he told her in a thickened voice as he stretched her quivering body out on the blanket he'd already spread. Before she could protest further, he was covering her body with his and pushing aside the lacy scraps of her bra. "No one will see us." His lips went once more to the hardened tips of her pink nipples and sucked gently as his fingers found the snap of her jeans.

"God, Laurie, you're so beautiful . . . so beautiful," he murmured. Unaccountably he felt her stiffen again, as though his compliment were unwelcome. But when his lips once more went to her swollen breasts and his hand slipped beneath the lacy waistband of the panties under her unzipped jeans, she sighed in surrender, and the tension he felt in her body had nothing to do with resistance.

With the fresh fragrance of grass beneath and the trees whispering softly around them, they were like the first lovers in paradise. When they came together, their fervent bodies entwined with an exalted urgency that seemed part of the rhythm of natural beauty that was its setting. When it was over, they lay exhausted, wrapped tightly in each other's arms and whispering words of endearment as they gazed up

132

through the lacy greenery to the heavenly vault of blue above and listened to the courting twitters of the birds.

"My God, Laurie, I've never felt anything like this before," Craig said huskily. "It's you. I can't keep my hands off you. I want to lose myself in your beauty."

There it was, that word again: "beauty." It had been intruding on her all day. Laurie sat up, suddenly self-conscious about her nakedness in this potentially exposed setting. Almost frantically she looked around for her scattered clothes. Seemingly puzzled by her sudden change of mood, Craig retrieved her bra and panties and then set about tugging on his own jeans and shirt.

When they both were set to rights, Laurie opened the basket they'd brought and began setting out the cheese, cold cuts, wine, and French bread she had packed.

As she made a show of busyness, Craig observed her with a slight frown tugging at his thick eyebrows. "Laurie," he finally asked, "is something wrong?"

She gave him a startled look and almost dropped the deviled eggs she was sliding onto a paper plate. "No, no, of course not."

"Were you embarrassed because I made love to you out in the open this way?" he inquired, ignoring her disclaimer. "If so, I'm sorry."

She shook her head, her eyes not quite meeting his. "No, it's not that. It was a wonderful experience, Craig. I'll treasure the memory always."

"Well then, what is it? I know something's bothering you."

She had loaded a plate with food for him, and as she handed him the dish along with a plastic cup filled with white wine, she shook her head emphatically. "It's nothing. Really! Let's drink to the day and just enjoy it."

133

He couldn't say no to that. So, grinning into her now hesitantly smiling eyes, he lifted his cup. "To the day and to us."

After the toast they enjoyed their meal. "Everything tastes delicious out in the open like this," Laurie commented.

"Just like you," Craig returned, winking at her as he helped pack away the basket and shake the grass from the blanket before folding it. "You taste delicious, and I'd better warn you that I'm probably going to want another bite when we get home."

She looked at him askance, one fine dark eyebrow arching. "I'm beginning to think you're insatiable."

"I plead guilty." As he took her elbow and guided her back down the path, Craig's grin was unrepentant. "When it comes to dishes like you, my appetite knows no bounds."

"And what sort of dish am I?"

Craig chuckled low in his throat. "A very delectable dishy dish. You're going to have to stop being so casual about your beauty and the effect it has on men. I'm not the only guy who's going to take one look and want to sink his teeth into your sweet flesh."

They had found the arboretum's exit and were headed toward the crest of the hilly street where Craig had parked his car. Though the afternoon had been warm and fair, the temperature had now dropped slightly, and a breeze had sprung up. It cut through the thin material of Laurie's blouse, chilling her. But she was chilled by more than the weather.

Last night and today had seemed perfect, but suddenly she was feeling less positive about the experience. "That didn't used to be a problem for me," she said carefully, watching as Craig stowed the picnic basket in the trunk and then opened the passenger door for her. "Men didn't used to want anything from me but help with a program or information on the latest computer hardware design. And that includes you, Craig."

He gave her a sharp look and then settled himself behind the wheel. "I'm talking about the way you are now. What you were in the past doesn't count."

Laurie twined her hands tightly in her lap and looked out the window. But as they drove down the winding residential street with its turn-of-the-century houses, she wasn't really seeing much. Her mind was too preoccupied with what Craig had said. All day she'd been having disquieting twinges at his references to her looks. So far she'd managed to disregard them. But now they'd come together in her mind in a fashion that was impossible to ignore. Unconsciously she began to gnaw her lower lip as her mind sifted through the facts troubling it. But it wasn't until they carried the blanket and picnic basket back into Craig's kitchen that she finally turned around to face him and spoke her mind.

"Why didn't I count in the past?"

He was unpacking the basket, and her question so startled him that he almost dropped the empty wine bottle. "What?"

"You said that what I was before didn't count. Why?"

He dumped the remaining debris into a large paper bag and then cast her a faintly irritated look. "Oh, for heaven's sake, you know perfectly well what I meant. Why are we wasting time on this?"

A knot seemed to tie itself in Laurie's chest. "Because all day, and last night, too, what you've said to me over and over is that I'm beautiful. Not that I'm fun to be with or that you like my smile or my conversation, but that I'm beautiful."

135

Craig gazed at her, his eyebrows slowly elevating. "You make it sound as though I've been insulting you. Women don't usually mind being told they're physically attractive. And in your case, it's certainly the truth. You're gorgeous, Laurie." His gaze warmed as it drifted over her, but in her present mood that disturbed her only more.

"Your compliments are bothering me because I've realized that in your mind my looks are all that's important." She stared back at him with a pained expression. "I'm no different from before. I don't think any differently or feel any differently. But my looks are altered, and for you that's the difference between night and day."

Craig had gone pale under his light tan, but now his skin began to flush, and his mouth compressed into a straight line. "Just what is it you're accusing me of? I always thought highly of you. I always appreciated your intelligence and your sense of humor. I always liked your conversation, your smile, your eyes."

All the doubt and resentment Laurie had been suppressing came to the fore in a rush. "Oh, sure. You thought I was okay to work with and even to be friends with. But never in your wildest dreams would you have made love to me the way you did this weekend. For the past twenty-four hours all you've done is admire my beauty—yes, beauty! I've gotten sick of hearing the word. But it's the key one for you, isn't it?" she said challengingly, her whole body beginning to tremble with the force of her feelings. "I've begun to realize that nothing else matters to you, and I've never felt so much like an object before in my life."

Like a stinging current, her hostile feelings had communicated themselves to Craig. Maybe he hadn't been telling her in the right way. But last night and today had been very special for him, and he felt hurt that she didn't seem to realize that. He had been genuinely caught up in Laurie's spell, and his praise of her beauty had been just a manifestation of his enthrallment. It had been a long time since he had felt this way about a woman. Now she appeared to be throwing his tender feelings back in his face. He was totally unprepared for what seemed like her unreasonable charge, and he couldn't stop himself from reacting with angry defensiveness.

"You never felt like an object before because you never had the chance. You can't have it both ways, Laurie. You can't make yourself unattractive and expect men to want you, and you can't make yourself beautiful and expect men not to notice and want you because of it. I think you're a very confused person," he added in a gentler voice.

But Laurie was too overwrought to appreciate his tone. Her eyes flashed dark fire. "Confused? Well, there's something I'm not confused about at all just now. Take me home, Craig Lawson. I want to leave this place right now!"

CHAPTER NINE

Sunday went by for Laurie in a haze of mental anguish. It was because Craig had appeared to care for her on more than just a physical level that she'd finally gone willingly to his bed. After that perfect night she'd begun to acknowledge how deep her feelings for him really were.

As she looked back, it seemed that she had just imagined his tender regard for her as a person. Almost as soon as they'd awakened in bed together, she'd sensed a change. By the end of the afternoon she'd known that he was treating her more like a prized object than a person for whom he really cared.

The thought made her clench her fists in something very close to physical pain. How could she have been so gullible? And how would she ever face Craig in the office on Monday?

It would be easier to hold her head up if she were the kind of modern woman who took her pleasure in bed without emotional commitment. But she wasn't that kind of person at all. And after that last acrimonious scene between Craig and her, he had to know it.

Under the circumstances working together from now on would be torture—at least for her. Yet they would have to manage somehow, at least for the time being. Although the basic problem with Archimedes had been solved, the details remained to be ironed out.

The fact was emphasized when Craig called her office almost the first thing that morning. "You may have forgotten, but I promised Penwaithe a full report on our Archimedes breakthrough before lunch. I can write something up myself, but I believe it will be stronger if it's a joint communiqué."

Although the thought of seeing Craig so soon made Laurie's stomach knot, she couldn't deny that what he said made sense. "All right," she said, trying to match the businesslike tone of his voice. "Do you want to work on it here, or shall I come up to your office?"

"Why don't you come up?" Though Craig sounded unemotional, Laurie knew that he also must be remembering what had happened in her office Friday evening—and later at his house.

"Certainly," she answered, beginning to gather up the manuals they'd need.

When she entered Craig's domain a half hour later, he was seated behind his broad walnut desk, thumbing through the Archimedes programming specifications. She closed the door and crossed to one of the blue easy chairs facing in his direction. But it was a full minute before he bothered to look up.

His failure to acknowledge her presence made her feel like a truant called into the principal's office. The cold expression in his green eyes when he finally did look up reinforced that impression.

"What took you so long?" he asked brusquely. "You know we're pressed for time on this."

Laurie shifted uncomfortably in the chair. Yet she was damned if she was going to let Craig Lawson buffalo her. "I

139

was marking some pertinent pages in the Hyohoto manuals," she explained. "I think in the long run that will expedite writing this report."

"You always were Miss Efficiency," he commented. And Laurie knew from the tone that he hadn't meant the observation as a compliment. What had happened to the man who'd done nothing but shower compliments on her all day Saturday? But she knew the answer to that question.

"Listen, Craig," she shot back, "you're the one who asked me to work on this with you." The moment the words were out of her mouth, she wished she could call them back. After the fireworks Saturday afternoon, getting into a verbal duel with him wasn't going to do her roiling stomach any good.

Apparently Craig had come to the same conclusion. "Then let's get to it," he muttered, turning to the computer terminal beside his desk. "It will be more efficient if you sit where you can see the screen, too," he added.

Pulling her chair around, Laurie positioned herself so that she was as far away from Craig as possible but still able to see the words he typed on his video display terminal. The irony of the situation wasn't lost on her. Friday night they'd been as close as possible—in his bed.

He shot her a derisive look. "Listen, I'm not going to molest you. So you can move where you're not going to give yourself eyestrain," he drawled.

Swallowing a sharp retort, Laurie moved a few inches closer and sat staring fixedly at the screen.

As Craig started the first paragraph, it seemed to Laurie that his fingers were hitting the keys with unnecessary force. But she certainly wasn't going to comment on that fact. However, she also wasn't going to let a report with her name on it go by with spelling and punctuation errors.

"Just a second," she said as his fingers flew over the keys. "You left an *s* out of 'insisted.' "

Craig moved the cursor up to correct the error.

"And you've got a comma splice in the sentence—or I guess I should say sentences—below that," she added.

"I prefer to get my thoughts down and edit later," Craig muttered. "But if you'd like to try another method, why don't you type?" he suggested, passing the keyboard to her.

Laurie looked down at the board and shook her head. "Your function keys are programmed differently from mine, so I'd just be wasting our time. I'm afraid you're going to have to do it."

Craig nodded curtly. But as he resumed typing, Laurie noticed that he went more slowly and seemed to be making an effort to reduce his errors.

The morning did not get easier as it progressed. By the time the report was finished Laurie and Craig were communicating mainly in not particularly friendly monosyllables.

It was a miracle that they'd been able to complete the document at all, Laurie thought as she left the promised material with Penwaithe's secretary.

By the time she returned to her own office it was noon. Glancing quickly at her watch, she considered calling Sandy about the lunch date her workload had postponed. But her hand hesitated as she reached for the telephone. Her sister was bound to ask about the weekend, and she just didn't feel like talking about it now. She certainly wasn't going to tell Sandy that she'd become a victim to her own absurd fantasies about Craig Lawson or that while she'd been falling under his spell even more deeply, he'd simply been amusing himself with her the way he might play with a new toy.

The thought made her stomach knot more tightly. There wasn't much use going to lunch anyway, she told herself.

She really didn't think she could choke down more than a cup of tea, which she could get from her secretary's hot plate.

Laurie was hoping things would be better the next day. Instead, they were worse. After reading the report, Penwaithe called a long meeting in which he insisted on ironing out several touchy points. The result was that she and Craig had to spend more time refining the material, which Penwaithe wanted circulated in the form of a memo.

That meant another work session alone with the man who was causing her so much emotional turmoil. By the end of the two tension-filled hours Laurie could barely keep her hands from trembling.

Even though their weekend of passionate lovemaking had unlocked the real meaning of her womanhood, she bitterly regretted the decision to let Craig become her lover. And he was obviously feeling the same disenchantment. The weekend had changed their whole relationship, but not for the better. Before, they had at least been friends. Now even that was ruined, and she had serious doubts about whether they could even work together effectively. If things went on like this, she might have to update her résumé and start sending it out.

During the next few days her state of mind did not improve. And depressing thoughts were still chasing themselves around in her troubled mind the next Monday evening, when Laurie pulled into the parking lot of the small supermarket a few blocks from her apartment building. She'd eaten next to nothing since the acrimonious scene with Craig, and nature was finally beginning to reassert itself. She was hungry for something substantial, and there was nothing tempting in her refrigerator. Often Laurie liked to enjoy a salad topped with tuna fish or hard-boiled eggs.

But this evening, as she headed for the produce department, she couldn't really work up any enthusiasm for canned fish and raw vegetables.

Maybe I'll just have some cheese on an English muffin, she thought, passing by the produce and threading her way down the aisle toward the bakery department. Suddenly she was hungry with a vengeance, feeling so empty that she was almost light-headed.

I could eat this whole shelf of stuff, she thought, pausing in front of an array of tempting-looking cakes and pies. The rich dark chocolate and artfully arranged whipped cream of a Black Forest cake caught her particular attention. Though she had been a chocolate addict, it had been a long time since she'd given in to the craving. Now the thought of that heavenly flavor combined with layers of cherry filling and whipped cream was so vivid that she could almost taste it.

Dragging her eyes away from the confection, she looked around resolutely for the English muffins. But when she located a package, somehow the nondescript flat muffins appeared about as tempting as hard-packed sand. Though she directed her hand to reach for the package, her gaze was pulled back to the cake. Suddenly all the willpower she'd been so proud of since she'd gone on her diet seemed to slip away like water down a drain.

Instead of closing on the package of English muffins, her hand veered away and reached for the square cake box. Quickly she deposited it in her cart. Then, in a sudden mood of defiance, she headed for the freezer department to buy a gallon of double chocolate ice cream.

"I've had enough of depriving myself in order to look good for creeps like Craig Lawson," she muttered under her breath as she dumped the ice cream into her cart and followed it with a frozen apple pie.

After hurriedly paying for her purchases, she drove home with the bag of forbidden goodies on the passenger seat next to her. From time to time she glanced at it with anticipation, imagining how much she was going to enjoy a dinner composed exclusively of the wonderful things she'd been denying herself. Her mind was so occupied with the enticing prospect that as she carried her bag into the lobby, she almost ran headlong into Art Frazier.

"Whoa!" he exclaimed, putting a hand on her shoulder to steady her. "What are you in such a rush about? I haven't seen you in more than a week."

Suddenly, as she eyed the tall blond, who was wearing white shorts and carrying a tennis racket, Laurie felt like a kid discovered with her hand in the cookie jar. Fortunately Art didn't really expect her to answer his question.

"I'm glad I bumped into you," he plowed on. "I've been meaning to ask if you'd like to check out the new disco on Main Street with me."

Laurie clutched her bag against her chest more tightly, suddenly embarrassed by its contents. "I'm not much of a dancer," she replied, and then remembered that she'd said something similar to Craig. Why did he always have to intrude in her thoughts? "And I've got to get this stuff upstairs and into the refrigerator," she added, a dismissive tone in her voice.

"Then let's talk about it some other time," Art said, shrugging and heading out toward the building's tennis court.

Laurie was aware that she'd been rude, but right now she wasn't in the mood to chastise herself for that. Instead, she stepped into the elevator, pushed the button for her floor, and leaned back against the wall, thinking about the secret gustatory treat she had arranged for herself. Life was tough enough without being denied the few small pleasures it offered, she rationalized as she closed her apartment door and strode toward the kitchen.

In only a few minutes she had cake and ice cream unpacked and was popping the pie in the oven to warm. *Let's start right off with the main event,* she told herself gleefully, cutting a giant slice of the Black Forest cake and topping it with several large dollops of chocolate ice cream.

Then she carried the heaping plate to the table in the kitchen and sat down. She swallowed the first three forkfuls of cake so quickly that she barely tasted them. But when she finally slowed down on the fourth bite, she really began to notice what was sliding over her palate. Laurie had been eating a healthy diet of fresh fruits and vegetables and other wholesome foodstuffs for so long that her tastes were much more acute than they'd been in the past.

Now the rich-looking confection, like most mass-produced bakery products, didn't live up to its luscious image. The whipped cream on top had a gummy texture and chemical aftertaste. The cake itself might as well have come from a box of ready-mix. Even the ice cream wasn't as good as she'd fantasized. It was too sweet, and the high fat content made it impossible for her to swallow more than a few bites before she began to feel overfull.

For a long moment she stared thoughtfully down at her partially eaten "meal." Then she pushed the plate away and sighed. "What am I doing?" she muttered aloud. "This is just the kind of stupid behavior I thought I'd overcome. Besides, this stuff doesn't even taste good anyway!"

Her crazy behavior was all Craig's fault, she thought. But then she brought herself up short. He really couldn't be blamed for her lapse. She was doing this to herself. She had let her feelings for him get out of hand. And that wasn't exactly his fault.

Laurie shook her head. Where was the mature, in-control woman she had thought herself?

Sighing again, she stood up and crossed to the window, where she looked out over the treetops and apartment tennis courts without really seeing them. The trouble was she was spending too much of her energy brooding over what had gone wrong between Craig and her. But he wasn't the only man in the world. Maybe the best way to get over him was to focus on someone else for a change. After all, she was still terribly inexperienced in matters of love. Maybe she was simply in the throes of an adolescent crush that most women would have outgrown long before now, and if she gave someone else a chance to engage her interest, the infatuation would dissipate.

The speculation made her think immediately of Art, whose lithe, athletic body she could see down at the practice wall below. He was a very attractive man who'd been pursuing her for weeks and had just asked her out, and she'd thoughtlessly turned him down for no good reason. Turning around, she took her plate to the sink and scraped the gooey cake and half-melted ice cream into the garbage disposal. Next, she flipped off the oven, pulled out the apple pie, and dumped it directly into the trash. Because of Craig, she'd rejected all of Art's friendly overtures. But that was ridiculous.

"Laurie, you're a fool," she said aloud. "You should have accepted the man's invitation. Now all you're going to do is sit home and worry yourself sick about Craig."

But was that really necessary? she asked herself. Art was downstairs now. What if she changed into shorts, went down to the courts, and asked for a lesson? Would he be as rude to her as she'd been to him? Or would he restate his invitation to go disco dancing? For a long moment she stood in the kitchen indecisively, wondering if she really wanted to do this. Then she squared her shoulders. The only way she was going to have a date with someone besides Craig was to take some positive action and announce her availability.

Twenty minutes later, dressed in a favorite racquetball outfit and with a pink sweatband holding back her dark hair, Laurie approached the high mesh fence enclosing the apartment building's tennis compound. Art was still there, slamming balls against the concrete practice wall. For a moment she paused to watch. And as she observed his skillful performance, she couldn't help comparing him to Craig.

Though Art was a blond, both men were similar physical types. They both were tall, lean, well muscled, and athletic. For a moment, as her gaze followed Art's masterful swing and well-coordinated footwork, her vision blurred, and she seemed to see him with much darker hair. Suddenly a picture of Craig as he had looked magnificently and unselfconsciously naked superimposed itself on the sunlit image before her. Her breath caught in her throat, and realizing what she was doing, she slammed an irritated fist into the palm of her opposite hand. Even now Craig Lawson was dominating her thoughts, and she simply couldn't continue this way.

It was then that Art noticed her. Turning, he let a ball go by and grinned. "Say, how long have you been there? I didn't see you."

"Only a few minutes," Laurie answered. "I've been watching you volley. You're very good."

His grin widened. "It's a lot more fun when I have someone to play with. How about a game?"

"I play racquetball, but I've never tried tennis."

Eagerly Art opened the gate and motioned her inside the practice area.

"Let me show you some basic strokes then," he said, handing her his racket and a tennis ball.

Laurie looked at the racket doubtfully. In comparison to the one she used on the indoor court at the athletic club, it looked large and unwieldy.

"I'll show you how to hold it," he said, coming around behind her and adjusting her hand on the grip. For the next half hour Laurie worked on forehands and backhands. Though Art was a good instructor, it was apparent that he was as much interested in having an excuse to touch her as in teaching her the game. When her very willing instructor draped an arm on her shoulder, Laurie couldn't help noticing what little effect the physical contact had. If Craig had done the same, she knew her nerve endings would be tingling from his touch. But Art might as well have been a brother. Physical contact with him left Laurie perfectly calm.

"Say," he asked as they strolled off the court, "how about that disco I mentioned? Do you want to give it a try this Friday?"

Laurie hesitated for only a second. "Sure," she said. Going out with a pleasant companion like Art was certainly better than staying home and moping about Craig.

Art beamed with pleasure, making Laurie wonder if she should have accepted his invitation. He might be expecting more from the evening than she was willing to give. But it was too late now to renege without looking like an utter idiot. "Great!" he was saying. "I'll pick you up at seven thirty."

It was partly defiance of Craig's attitude and partly a wish to please Art with her appearance, if nothing else, that made Laurie spend a lot of time preparing for their date. She even went out and bought a dress she thought would be appropriate for the occasion. It was a silvery sheath with spaghetti straps and an almost thigh-high slit up one leg for mobility. Her eye makeup, too, was silver accented by a smoky blue. As she stepped back from the mirror, she was pleased by the way it made her eyes seem even darker and more luminous than usual. Her hair also pleased her. She had tried various styles but finally settled on holding her sable tresses back with combs and letting them tumble in a dusky waterfall down her back.

When she opened the door to Art, he was obviously very taken with her dramatic costume.

"Wow!" he exclaimed. "You really are a knockout. I can't wait to show you off out on the dance floor!"

It was then that a horrible thought struck Laurie. Somehow she had been concentrating so hard on accepting this date that she hadn't given much thought to the practical reality of the evening. Earlier she'd told Craig that she wasn't very good at dancing. And it was absolutely true. In fact, she'd never been to a disco and hadn't the slightest idea what was expected.

However, when Art did lead her onto the strobe-lit floor of Storm Warnings, the new club near the campus, Laurie breathed a sigh of relief. All the dancers around her were doing their own thing. Basically it wasn't much different from the kinds of steps she'd learned in her aerobics class. In a few minutes she felt quite at home with the music and the other dancing couples.

"This is fun," she told Art during one of the brief breaks in the music. It really was fun. *Just what I needed,* Laurie admitted to herself as she and Art got up for another energetic set. The old Laurie would have been exhausted after fifteen minutes, she mused. But now she merely felt exhilarated by the frenetic activity.

"You're really terrific on the dance floor," Art said complimentarily as they headed back to his car. "We'll have to do this again real soon."

Laurie wasn't sure how to answer that. She'd enjoyed the evening, but she didn't want to lead Art on. The way he was looking at her made it obvious that he wouldn't settle for a platonic friendship. Yet aside from the dancing, she hadn't found that they had very much in common. Art's small talk was mostly from the newspaper's sports pages. Though he asked about her work, he didn't seem particularly interested in her answers.

He was, however, interested in kissing her good night. It was also clear, when they paused in front of her door, that he wanted to be invited in. Since Laurie had no intention of acceding to that request, she decided to opt for the lesser of the two evils.

Lifting her face to Art's, she waited with a certain amount of curiosity to see what would happen. When his lips met hers, the warm, firm pressure was very pleasant. Art's technique, she noted with the detachment of a scientist watching an experiment, was every bit as good as Craig's. Yet when the kiss finally ended, she was neither trembling nor breathless. The chemistry simply wasn't there. Art apparently didn't affect her the way Craig invariably did.

But Art's reaction wasn't the same as hers. "Why don't you ask me in for a nightcap?" he asked huskily. As he spoke, his fingers played with one of the combs in her hair.

She was about to repeat her original negative when a flutter of movement a few paces down the hall caught her eye.

It was Craig stepping out of the shadows by the stairway, a rigid expression on his features as he took in her gleaming outfit and cozy proximity to her tall, good-looking date.

"Laurie has no intention of inviting you in, fella," he rasped, "so why don't you just run along?"

Art whirled, unable to suppress a startled exclamation. "What the—"

Craig stepped forward, clamped a possessive hand on Laurie's arm, and faced the other man squarely. "I said, run along," he repeated.

For a moment Art stared in astonishment before shooting Laurie a questioning look. At first she was so surprised by Craig's behavior that she couldn't respond. But then, realizing the explosive potential of the situation, she nodded at her escort.

"I guess it would be better if you left," she told Art, giving him a pleading look. But though she managed to remain relatively calm, she was inwardly seething with fury at the other man's high-handed behavior. What right did he have to interfere in her life this way? she asked herself, watching Art shrug and then amble off down the hall.

He seemed to be taking this interference with a remarkable amount of good grace. But just before disappearing into the elevator, he turned and grinned at his date. "You were great tonight, Laurie. Holding you in my arms was as exciting as holding silver lightning—and I'm glad you enjoyed it as much as I did." He paused, and his smile widened. "We'll do it again really soon, and that's a promise!"

The words were obviously meant not for her, but for the rather aggressive interloper who had soured his plans for the rest of the evening. And they had the desired effect. Craig's eyes narrowed, and for a moment he seemed about to start down the hall after the other man. But Art was apparently playing it safe. After delivering his salvo, he stepped quickly into the elevator, and the doors whooshed closed behind him.

Laurie was left alone with Craig in the empty corridor.

"I presume you don't want to discuss this in the hall," he snarled between his teeth as he lifted the key from her hand and inserted it in the lock.

"I don't want to discuss it at all," she said.

But Craig gave her little opportunity to protest. In the next moment the door swung open and he was marching her inside.

"All right, what's the big idea?" he asked.

Laurie's mouth dropped open. "I think that's my line," she responded. "Where do you get off playing a scene like that with one of my neighbors?"

"Oh, yeah, you were just being neighborly, I suppose." Craig snorted. Laurie had seen him irritated over problems in the office, but she had never seen him in this sort of temper. His eyes had the dangerous look of radioactive emeralds. And the rigid set of his shoulders made her think of a bull about to charge.

However, she was angry, too, and faced him without outwardly flinching.

"You have no right—" she said.

Craig wasn't about to let her finish. "Don't talk about rights," he told her. "Last week you were a shivering virgin in my bed. The next day you let me make love to you in the arboretum. This week—this week you're dressed like a hooker," he said, waving an accusing hand at her glittering silver dress. "And," he barreled on, his temper completely out of control, "it sounds as if you're letting that overgrown jock screw you."

It was now Laurie's dark eyes that flashed fire, yet she

152

forced her next words to sound deadly calm. "In the first place"—she enunciated carefully—"this dress is perfectly appropriate for a night of disco dancing. And in the second place, that's all Art and I were doing, nothing more."

Craig took a step forward and put his hands on her shoulders as though he wanted to shake her. "Well, dancing may be all you were doing *this time.* But from the tender scene I witnessed at the door, that guy Art has something a lot more basic in mind. And you didn't look all that unwilling yourself." He paused for a moment. "Just tell me this. Do you intend to keep on seeing him?"

Actually Laurie had already decided that she didn't want any more involvement with Art. But Craig's imperious tone fueled her defiance. Tossing her head back so that her long hair lashed her shoulders, she glared up at him.

"That's none of your business. I'll see whatever man I want to—and do whatever I want to with him."

Craig's skin flushed a shade darker, and his hands tightened painfully on her shoulders. "You walked out on me last week because you said I was obsessed by your looks. Well, what do you think it is about you that attracts that palooka? Do you think he would have given you the time of day a year ago when you were"—he stopped and eyed her delicate frame—"fifty pounds heavier and looking like a brunette Miss Piggy?"

Laurie's response to the deliberate insult was automatic. Her hand shot up, and she slapped Craig across the face with a satisfying crack that left the imprint of her fingers on his cheek.

For a moment he looked stunned. And Laurie wondered if he might retaliate in kind. Instead, he took a step backward.

"Christ, Laurie, I'm sorry. That was a rotten thing to say."

"Yes," she said, turning her back to him so that he wouldn't see the stricken expression she knew was in her eyes. "Now will you please get out of here?"

"Laurie," he said appealingly, trying to touch her shoulder, "if you understood why I came here, you wouldn't send me away now."

But she only shook his hand off and took a step away.

"If you have any decency at all, please leave," she repeated in frigid tones.

For a moment there was only silence behind her. And then she heard him sigh heavily. The next sound was the careful closing of the door as he left.

Her apartment was empty, completely empty. And suddenly she felt like the loneliest person in the world.

Craig climbed into his car and pounded his fist against the steering wheel. God, he had acted like an idiot up there. He wouldn't be surprised if Laurie refused to see him again. And he couldn't blame her. He had only himself to blame for that juvenile performance.

Though what he had said to her in anger about Art's motives was doubtlessly accurate, what she'd said to him last week about his own motives was even more telling. It was natural to be attracted to a woman with Laurie's looks. But there were things that were much more important than mere beauty. Unlike Art, he'd had an opportunity to recognize those qualities in Laurie. In fact, they'd drawn him to her even before she'd lost all that weight.

What a fool he'd been to overlook that attraction, he thought in self-castigation.

Sighing, he started the car and pulled out of the parking

space. In his mind was the parade of vapid beauties he'd been squiring all these years since his disillusioning divorce. He had dated them more because they flattered his own ego than because he enjoyed being with them. And if he were really honest, he would have to admit the same had been true of his wife. Although he'd harbored a lot of resentment toward her and the institution of marriage itself, their union had really failed because they'd had nothing in common besides her good looks and his admiration of them. He'd never really loved her, he admitted, never really loved anyone before, perhaps because he'd never been taught how to.

Then all at once it came to him: What he felt for Laurie was so different from what he'd felt for any other woman that it must be love. That was why he had been tied up in knots all week and had made an utter ass of himself tonight outside her apartment door.

Craig shook his head and sighed again. What a fine time it was to realize that he loved her—when it looked as if he'd ruined everything.

The dark, deserted street seemed to accentuate his present mood. It was time for some soul-searching if it wasn't already too late.

CHAPTER TEN

The ringing of the phone dragged Laurie from a restless sleep. Who would be calling so early? she wondered irritably. But when she glanced at the clock on the bedside table, she saw that it was already ten thirty.

She'd been up pacing the floor over the scene with Craig the night before so that she hadn't gotten to sleep till the wee hours of the morning. For a moment she was tempted to pull the covers over her head and ignore the insistent ringing. What if it were Craig? But Laurie had never been able to ignore a jangling phone for long. After reaching out from under the blanket, she picked up the receiver.

"I was afraid you might have gone out," Sandy's cheerful voice chirped over the line.

Laurie's heart sank. She realized that irrational though it might be, she had really been wishing it would be Craig. Was she hoping that he'd apologize? Or did she want another chance to say the acrimonious things that hadn't come to mind last night but had been running through her head ever since? She didn't know. In fact, she couldn't say *what* she wanted from the man anymore.

"Sis? Are you there?" Sandy's voice jarred her from her reflections. "Don't tell me I woke you so early in the morning. Aren't you usually the early bird?"

"Sorry," Laurie answered. "I guess my mind was wandering?"

"Wandering?" Sandy picked up immediately on the plaintive note in the younger woman's voice. "You sound as if you've been up all night worrying about something."

Laurie sighed. "Why do you always have to be so damn perceptive?"

Her sister chuckled. "For one thing, it's my job. And for another, I know you've been avoiding me, so I assume something's gone wrong between you and Craig—and I'm nosy enough to want to know what it is."

"How do you know it's gone wrong?" Laurie asked, sitting up on her futon and propping her back against the wall.

"Because if you had had anything positive to report, I would have heard it by now. Listen, I'm alone in the house," she went on quickly. "Frank and the kids are off on the first —yuck—fishing expedition of the year. So why don't you come over and spend the morning with me, or the whole day, if you don't have other plans?"

Laurie was about to issue an automatic refusal when she reconsidered. Maybe it would be a good thing to get out and see a friendly face. Besides, if she could just bring herself to talk about the mess she was in, Sandy would be able to add a disinterested perspective. She had always respected her sister's judgment even when she initially resisted her conclusions. "All right," she said. "I'll be there as soon as I can get ready."

"Then plan on brunch. You've inspired me to try some low-cal recipes, and I'd like to see what you think of them."

Laurie laughed. "You don't have to do any more of a selling job." She hesitated for a moment and then plunged ahead. "Listen, there *is* something I do want to talk to you about. But I might lose my nerve by the time I get there. Don't let me, okay?"

There was a moment of silence on the other end of the line. "Sounds mysterious. Now that you've dropped that little hook, you'd better hurry over."

Thirty minutes later Laurie was sitting at the Campana kitchen table, watching her sister separate eggs. "Wait till you taste this cheese puff," Sandy said braggingly. "Of course, my thrifty soul hates throwing out half the yolks. But when I remember that I'm throwing out all the cholesterol and almost all the calories, I can force myself to do it."

As Laurie sipped her coffee and tried to get up the nerve to raise the subject of Craig, Sandy grated low-cal cheese and cut bread cubes for the dish.

"Listen," her sister said, "I haven't forgotten that you want to have a serious talk. But I'm not going to make you do it on an empty stomach."

"Thanks." Laurie leaned back in her chair and stretched out her legs. She had forgotten how comfortable it was to spend a morning with her older sister.

But she got less comfortable after eating the delicious cheese puff her sister had prepared. When both their dishes were empty, Sandy pushed back her plate, refilled her coffee cup, and gave her a direct look.

"Okay, let's have it," she ordered.

Laurie grinned nervously. "Well, brunch was delicious. But I've already told you that."

"As I recall, you told me not to let me off the hook."

"Yes." Laurie sighed. "You're right. But that doesn't make it any easier." She took a deep breath and then, wrapping her fingers tightly around her coffee cup, plunged ahead. In a few minutes, without going into the intimate

158

details of her weekend with Craig, she outlined the ups and downs their relationship had taken in the past few weeks.

When she finished her narrative, Sandy was looking at her with a mixture of concern and doubt. "It sounds as if you've been going through hell," she said sympathetically, "and I think I can understand your feelings, at least partly. But I have to add that in a lot of ways I agree with Craig. You *are* confused. And I'd guess he's been going through hell, too."

Feeling betrayed, Laurie scraped back her chair and stood up. "Well, if that's all the help I'm going to get from you, I might as well go home."

"Calm down," Sandy said soothingly. "You don't want me just to cluck and agree with you. You came for some advice, and you're going to get it."

"Even if I don't want to hear it?"

"Yes. It's time for good old Dr. Campana, your friendly campus counselor, to take center stage. Forget that I'm your sister. I'm going to treat you the way I would any young woman who came to me with a problem like yours. The only difference is that we're not going to take weeks working through your feelings. This will be the short course. And there's no charge."

Reluctantly Laurie sat back down. "Are you on my side or not?" she asked challengingly.

"I told you I was. But I have to be on Craig's side, too, because I don't think you're being fair to him. Honey, he's a man. Men are attracted to good-looking women. That's the way Mother Nature arranged things, you know."

"But that's all he's attracted to," Laurie said in protest.

Sandy shook her head. "Do you really believe that?" she asked. "And if you do, how about yourself? Let's face it, Craig is a fantastic-looking guy. Why do you think you have it bad for him, not for some pale and paunchy physics professor?"

"Because Craig and I have a lot in common," Laurie answered quickly. "We're both computer professionals. We both like sports. And we laugh at the same sort of things." She didn't go on to describe how much pleasure they'd found in each other's arms, yet it was in her mind.

"But think about what first attracted you to him, Laurie. Are you going to tell me it was the way he programmed his computer?"

"Maybe it was his sense of humor," Laurie said.

"So, Rodney Dangerfield is a very funny man. Do you want a relationship with him?"

Laurie glared at her sister. "What are you trying to prove anyway?"

"I'm just trying to get you to look at this fairly. Maybe you could develop a loving relationship with a man who looked like Rodney Dangerfield. But you have to admit his appearance wouldn't get things started on the fast track. And I think if you're honest with yourself, you'll concede that it's a lot easier to get to know someone who attracts you physically. For the relationship to last, there has to be more than that, of course. But it sure does make a great beginning."

Laurie stared at her sister in silence for a moment. "I think I'd better go home," she finally managed to say.

Sandy cocked her head. "I know I've been hard on you, but it's for your own good."

"Sure."

"Just promise me one thing. Don't go home mad. Go home and think about it."

For the next week that was exactly what Laurie did. The frank conversation was on her mind every day as she went into the office, and her thoughts were still dwelling on it when she went home at night. What would she say to Craig the next time she saw him? she asked herself. While she was at work, she was constantly on the alert, expecting to run into him at any moment. But after a few days she began to wonder why she wasn't seeing him. Was he avoiding her?

The question was answered when his secretary called to cancel a meeting. "Mr. Lawson is out of town on vacation this week and next," she added. "When he returns, I'll call to reschedule."

Laurie's eyebrows shot up. So that was why she hadn't seen him around. Did his "vacation" have anything to do with that scene in her apartment? she wondered. It was hard to believe that their arguments had upset him as much as her. Yet he hadn't said anything about going away before, and that he would leave so precipitously was too much of a coincidence.

This new development gave her something else to think about, and she was mulling it over when she went downstairs for a late lunch. She was so preoccupied that she almost bumped into an attractive young man dressed in a light blue suit who was just turning away from the salad bar.

"Ms. DiMaria," he said enthusiastically, "I was hoping I'd bump into you—not literally, of course."

Laurie's mouth dropped open as she realized who he was. "Buddy?" she asked, taking in his neatly razor-cut hair, the contact lenses that had replaced his glasses, and his trimmer figure.

"It's me all right." He grinned, in answer to her confounded expression. Laurie could tell he was enjoying the moment. *And rightfully so,* she told herself. He looked like a different person—not only trimmer but more poised and confident.

"What happened to you?" she asked as she walked alongside him with her tray. When they found an empty table and sat down together, he explained.

"Actually I took your advice. For the past five weeks I haven't just been dieting; I've been exercising, reading books, and buying new clothes. I never felt so good in my life."

Laurie looked across the table at him approvingly. To her surprise she felt almost as proud of his transformation as he did himself. "Well, all that hard work shows. You've done wonders with yourself. I didn't even recognize you at first."

Buddy's smile widened. "I know. Isn't it great? And it's made a big difference in my social life, too. Girls I wouldn't have had the nerve even to talk to a month ago are starting up conversations with *me*. Boy, am I ever glad I signed up for that counseling seminar. Ms. Campana did a great job, but it was really your talk about yourself that inspired me."

Laurie didn't know what to say. She was touched. "I'm glad I made a difference," she finally murmured. They chatted amiably through lunch, and she found herself treating Buddy more as an equal than she had in the past.

That evening, as she fixed a light supper, both Craig and Buddy were on Laurie's mind. The change in the formerly unattractive younger man was still startling to her. Before, she hadn't been able to imagine him appealing to pretty coeds; now it seemed entirely possible. Yet, she mused, as she chopped parsley and scallions for her omelet, the change in Buddy was much less radical than the change in herself. He hadn't had time to lose more than ten or fifteen pounds, whereas she'd spent a year shedding a good quarter of her weight. Furthermore, she'd had the advantage of a full year of exercise, plus being able to use makeup and a new wardrobe to change her look.

The realization made her thoughts turn to Craig. She was reacting differently to Buddy because of his altered appearance. It might not be fair, but somehow she had more respect for the well-groomed young man she'd met today than for the pudgy, rumpled-looking guy who'd signed up for Sandy's seminar. Irrational though she knew it to be, he even seemed more capable and intelligent now.

Well, if she could react that way to someone like Buddy, who was after all only a casual acquaintance, what about Craig's changed feelings for her? He had told her he'd liked her before her weight loss. But he hadn't entertained any romantic feelings toward the woman she'd appeared to be. How could she blame him for encouraging their friendship to blossom into something more when she reappeared in his life with a new, attractive body? Sandy had been right after all. She wasn't being fair to the man.

The realization made her anxious to talk to Craig. She wanted to apologize for her hasty words. But it was more than that. During the weekend they'd spent together, she'd ended up infusing so much negative meaning into his words of praise for her transformed physical appearance that she'd ignored the reality of his actions. He hadn't even tried to bed her until she'd expressed herself as more than willing. Then his lovemaking had been tender, gentle, and considerate. No woman could have asked for a sweeter lover or a more moving first experience.

Surely that wasn't all merely expertise he'd learned with other women. Such restraint and consideration had to stem from his feelings for her as a person—not just another bed partner. And she had walked over those feelings roughshod because of her own insecurities. He and Sandy had diagnosed her problem correctly. She was confused, and she needed to start thinking clearly for a change.

But that was more easily said than done. When they'd fought, she'd been too obsessed with her own point of view to give any real credence to Craig's. What's more, there were her own strong feelings for him to consider. They hadn't gone away because she'd doubted his sincerity. If anything, they were even more painful now than they'd been before.

What was she going to do? she asked herself, unconsciously wringing her hands. It was impossible to sort out the problems in their relationship—if they still had one, that is—without Craig's help. She needed to talk to him, and to do that, she'd have to swallow her pride and find out where he'd gone.

Getting in touch with him, though, proved to be more difficult than she'd anticipated. When she called his secretary the next day at work to find out his vacation address, the woman informed her coolly, "Mr. Lawson has given me strict instructions not to give out that information."

Laurie was flabbergasted. "Are you certain? This is Ms. DiMaria. I'm sure he wouldn't object to my knowing where he is."

"I'm sorry. He was very firm on the issue. He insisted that this was one vacation when he didn't want to be disturbed—by anyone," she added.

Laurie drummed her nails on the desk. "But someone at the company would have to be able to locate him in an emergency. Does Mr. Penwaithe have his address?"

A slight hesitation gave the truth away as far as Laurie was concerned. "I'm sorry, I can't discuss that," the secretary finally said. But she didn't need to discuss it. Laurie knew how to get in touch with Craig now.

But how to go about it? she wondered. She certainly couldn't tell Penwaithe the real reason why she needed to see Craig. The request would have to be put in the form of a professional inquiry. Fortunately that subterfuge turned out to be unnecessary.

When, ten minutes later, she entered Penwaithe's plushly carpeted outer office, it was deserted, his secretary having presumably gone out for coffee. What's more, the door to the inner sanctum was firmly shut. All Laurie had to do was turn the receptionist's revolving phone directory around and flip it to the L's. At the bottom of Craig's card was a penciled-in address on Michigan's Upper Peninsula. Laurie remembered that he'd once told her about inheriting some property on the lakeshore up there from a distant uncle who didn't have any other heirs.

Quickly she copied down the information and stuffed it into her jacket pocket. But when she was back in her office staring at the scrap of paper with Manistique written on it, she wasn't sure how to proceed. Though she'd lived in Michigan most of her life, she'd never visited its fabled Upper Peninsula. A quick look at the map in the office atlas showed her why. It was at least a two-day drive to the place where Craig had isolated himself.

Laurie tapped her finger thoughtfully against the map. Even if she drove all the way up, he might not even be there when she arrived.

For the rest of the day these facts were in the back of her mind as she tried to concentrate on getting something done in the office. By that evening she'd made up her mind. She wasn't really getting a thing accomplished at work and was driving herself crazy to boot. Better to do something than just wait around stewing like this.

Luckily the Archimedes project no longer needed her constant attention. And she had vacation time coming. It was a simple matter to make arrangements for a week away from the office. Once that was done, it remained only to let Sandy know where she was going and pack her things.

"Gee, it's good to hear from you!" her older sister exclaimed over the phone. "I was afraid I'd been too hard on you this time."

"No," Laurie said reassuringly. "You were right. But it took me almost a week to come to that conclusion. Craig's at Manistique on the Upper Peninsula. I've decided to go up there to talk to him."

"Good for you," Sandy said approvingly. "And good luck. I hope everything works out the way you want it to."

I hope so, too, Laurie thought as she finished loading the trunk of her car for the trip. Glancing back, she noticed that Art Frazier was down at the tennis court again, practicing his stroke. He hadn't spoken to her or even waved, and she had a strong suspicion that it was because of the nasty scene with Craig. She certainly couldn't blame him. And she suddenly felt she couldn't leave without apologizing.

When she approached the court, her former date gave her a wary look and shook his head. "Did Godzilla leave you off the chain long enough to speak to me?" he inquired dryly.

Laurie had the grace to flush. "Art, I'm sorry that happened. Craig and I'd had a fight, and he wasn't himself."

The tall blond didn't look particularly mollified. "Oh, you mean you were just going out with me to spite him?"

It sounded horrible, but there was an element of truth in his accusation. "It's not as bad as that. I like you, and I enjoyed our date."

Art swung his racket in a half loop. "But no bells and whistles went off when I kissed you, did they?"

Ruefully Laurie shook her head. "I'm in love with Craig," she said aloud, realizing that it was the first time she'd actually voiced the admission.

Art shrugged and slammed a ball solidly against the cement practice wall. "Well, then go for it!" he admonished her over his shoulder.

"Thanks, I will," Laurie responded before heading back toward her car and climbing into the driver's seat. Taking a deep breath, she started the engine. She'd never made a drive like this by herself before. And she was a little afraid of the long hours behind the wheel.

But after she'd gotten past the more populated areas of the state, she found herself enjoying Michigan's spectacular scenery, much of it still unspoiled. Deep green trees accented by sparkling lakes lined the route she'd chosen. As she pushed northward, she began to feel as though she were leaving the twentieth century behind and actually driving into Paul Bunyan country.

She spent the night in a rustic cabin overlooking a lake near Maple Valley. The next morning she headed out toward the magnificent Straits of Mackinac which joined lakes Huron and Michigan. As a child she'd swum in Lake Huron, of course. But she'd never really appreciated its size until she saw it from the spectacular five-mile suspension bridge that joined the Upper Peninsula to the rest of the state.

Once on the other side of the straits, she headed along the coast of Lake Michigan toward Manistique. But now she was much less able to appreciate the rugged beauty of the stunning scenery. What if this all were a wild-goose chase? What if Craig weren't there? Worse, what if he were there and didn't want to see her?

It was late afternoon by the time she'd reached the outskirts of the quaint little town where he was supposed to be staying. To her surprise, she was greeted by a forty-foot statue of Paul Bunyan himself. Shaking her head, she grinned as she drove past. When she'd been fantasizing about the giant woodsman, she hadn't really expected to encounter him in person.

Driving through town, Laurie looked around for a motel. There were several on Route 2, and after she'd checked into a clean-looking place done in white clapboard and overlooking the beach, she collapsed onto the wide double bed, closed her eyes, and thought about her strategy.

What if Craig weren't here after all? she asked herself again. Then all this trouble had just been for nothing. It had been crazy to jump in the car and come all this way without calling first. But she simply hadn't been able to picture herself talking about their problems on the phone. The thought made her want to get up and check out the address she'd written down in Ann Arbor. But she was just too tired. It would simply have to wait until she'd caught a nap and taken a shower.

Evening shadows were already beginning to lengthen in the room when Laurie awoke from a deeply disturbing dream. It had started with her in Craig's arms. They were making love. She could remember vividly the sensation of his naked skin on hers. He'd brought her close to the peak of passion with his hands and lips, but when she'd reached out to pull his body on top of hers, he'd drawn back. Suddenly they weren't in his bedroom anymore. She'd seen herself fighting her way through smothering veils of mist. Craig had been just ahead, only faintly visible through the gloom. And when she'd called out to him, he'd turned away and disappeared.

For a long moment after she wakened, she lay trembling as she remembered her dream. It paralleled her waking fears closely. *But that won't happen,* she told herself. *Surely Craig will give me a hearing when I go to see him.*

168

Glancing at her watch, she was surprised to see how late it was. Had she slept so long and had that horrible dream because she was afraid to face what lay ahead? It would be impossible to barge in on Craig now. But there might still be time at least to locate his cottage.

A hot shower made her feel better. After changing into clean clothes, Laurie headed for the small restaurant attached to the hotel and fortified herself with a bowl of fish chowder and a salad. When she'd paid for her light meal, she pulled out Craig's address and showed it to the hostess.

"Could you tell me where to find West Beach Road?" she inquired.

"Sure," the woman answered pleasantly. "It's about eight miles from here, on the other side of town. There's a grocery store at the corner—you can't miss it."

The hostess had been right. West Beach Road was easy to find, but once she'd turned off onto the narrow gravel lane, the houses were few and far between, and the road was lit only by moonlight. In the gathering twilight it was sheer luck that she managed to catch a glimpse of Craig's name on the mailbox as she drove past a cedar shake bungalow set back from the road and screened by pines.

Laurie pulled the car to the dusty shoulder and tapped her fingers on the steering wheel. *What now?* she asked herself. As she debated her next move, a light went on in the front of the house. Her heart skipped a beat, and her eyes focused eagerly on the brightness. Craig was home. If she could find the courage, it would be possible to talk to him tonight.

Laurie could now see into a room comfortably furnished with overstuffed chairs and a leather couch. But it was not the furniture she saw. It was the figure of a man that captured her attention. At this distance through the trees he was hard to make out. Even so, she knew it was Craig.

The sight of his lean masculine form made her heart lurch again inside her chest. Suddenly all the confused feelings that had been churning around inside her since their weekend of passionate lovemaking were crystallized. What had she been thinking of? She loved this man, had loved him for a long time. Yet she'd turned him away—twice. How she regretted that blind stupidity now! Was it too late to tell him how she felt? A tear ran down Laurie's cheek as she gazed through the darkness. She couldn't let something this important go until tomorrow, Laurie realized. She had to talk things over with Craig tonight.

Opening the door of the car, she swung her feet out and started up the gravel drive. But instead of going directly to the door, she was drawn to the lighted window where she'd spied Craig.

As she approached, she could make out his features more clearly. He was staring out into the darkness as though he were hoping to find the answer there to some important question. For a heart-stopping moment she was almost sure he could see her. His green eyes seemed to be looking directly into hers, as though he could penetrate into her soul. Her hand flew to her mouth. For a flash of time, as if he were holding her fast, she was unable to move. Then she reminded herself that her little fantasy was impossible. There was no way his gaze could pierce the darkness from a lighted room.

Somewhat reassured, she tiptoed closer. The expression on his face made her draw in her breath sharply. It was not the look of dreamy introspection one might expect on a warm night in June. Instead, it was a mask of anger. As she watched in fascination, he clenched his jaw and then drew his right hand into a fist and smashed it into the opposite palm. The window was open, and she could hear the sound of his furious gesture. Was he thinking of her? she wondered, drawing back with a shiver. Suddenly she was certain that he was.

The notion sent another icy tremor through her, and all the courage she'd mustered since her disturbing afternoon dream seemed to evaporate. With sagging shoulders, she turned and tiptoed back down the gravel drive. As she'd walked toward his cottage, she'd been imagining how it would feel to have Craig's arms around her again, to crush her womanly softness to his masculine strength. Now that was unthinkable. The two long, tiring days of driving had been for nothing. She might as well turn around and go home.

The abortive encounter had drained the last of Laurie's strength. When she returned to her motel, she was not able to do anything more than pull off her clothes and crawl into bed. She was even too tired to weep. That would come later, when she had really come to grips with what she had lost.

One thing was sure: She couldn't stay here. In the morning she would check out and go back to Ann Arbor, she thought as she closed her eyes in exhaustion and sought refuge in unconsciousness.

CHAPTER ELEVEN

•

Luckily things can seem different on a beautiful sunlit morning. As Laurie looked out the window at the bright blue water sparkling beyond the strip of pale sand that lined the beach, she realized that she wasn't yet ready to carry out the anguished decision she'd made last night.

However, coming to that conclusion didn't calm her nervous stomach. After scanning the menu in the little restaurant adjacent to the motel, she knew she wouldn't be able to choke down a thing. It was all she could do to swallow a cup of tea before wandering down to the nearby beach.

I haven't driven all the way up here to turn tail and run, she told herself as she sat down on a driftwood log to look at the waves roll gently in. For a few moments she simply watched the gentle swells that broke against the sand with almost hypnotic regularity. The height of the waves and the broad expanse of water made it hard to imagine that she was really on the shore of a lake. There was no land in sight on the horizon. As long as she kept her gaze forward, she could pretend that she was on a deserted island in the middle of a limitless ocean.

But when she got up to stroll slowly down the driftwood-strewn beach, the pine forest off to her right reminded her where she was. After last night's clandestine visit to Craig's cottage, at least one thing was clear: She was in love with him. And she didn't want to give him up—unless she had to.

Why had she jumped to the conclusion that he was angry with her? she asked herself. He might have been thinking of almost anything unpleasant. Even if he were irritated with her, she would simply have to break through that mood. They had to have this out. In fact, she wouldn't be able to do anything constructive at work or in her personal life until they did.

But since Craig wasn't even aware that she was here, she would have to approach him. How should she do it? she wondered. For a moment her gaze swept out over the water again. Then an idea struck her, and she began to walk quickly back toward her car. She'd noticed a beachwear store on the main street. There had been a number of bikinis in the window that would be perfect for her purposes.

Forty-five minutes later she was back in her motel room, taking the tags off a daringly brief scarlet bathing suit. The strips of bright cloth had been labeled "Candy Apple." And the whimsy of that color designation had prompted her selection. A week ago she would never have had the nerve to wear something like this in public. But maybe it was time to have an unveiling, she thought as she quickly shed her cutoffs and T-shirt.

A few moments later she stood before the full-length mirror on the bathroom door, inspecting her scantily clad image. Her gaze ran down from the sweep of night black hair brushing her shoulders to the small, perfectly formed breasts covered by scraps of brilliant cloth. Their shape was emphasized, rather than hidden, by the flaming fabric. Her gaze traveled farther down to her narrow waist and the flat plane of her stomach, and then lower to the merest triangle of scarlet that did little to protect her modesty. Although the expanse of skin she could see was not yet tan, its smooth olive texture was set off perfectly by the contrast with the Candy Apple excuse for a bathing suit.

With a little shake of her head Laurie admitted that she liked what she saw. All this time she'd been struggling with the physical changes her body had undergone during the last year. It had been hang-ups about her "real self" that had caused so many of her problems with Craig. Finally, she had come to terms with all that. By wearing this bathing suit, she was certainly proving that she no longer felt ill at ease about her body. This was her new physical presence. And she was finally comfortable with it.

Would Craig recognize the statement? she asked herself as she turned away from the mirror and reached for her terry cover-up, sunglasses, and wide-brimmed straw hat. It was hard to believe that he wouldn't understand the gesture—or respond to its provocation.

Twenty minutes later, as she pulled up near Craig's cottage, she felt less certain of her bold plan. It was one thing to parade around practically nude in the privacy of her motel room. It was quite another to prance around like this on a public beach. But maybe she wouldn't have to, she decided, looking up to make sure that his car was still in the driveway. If he was at home, they could talk in his living room.

But though she knocked on the door several times, there was no answer. Was Craig out in back or walking on the beach? she wondered, making her way around the side of the shingled cottage. It was then that she spotted him about a hundred yards away. He was sitting on a driftwood log, facing the broad expanse of the lake much as she had earlier that morning.

To judge from the way his chin rested on his fist, his

thoughts were a million miles away. Laurie stood watching him uncertainly. A feeling of lonely isolation about his pose struck her like a blow. Should she accost him? He looked so unapproachable. This didn't seem the right time to get through to the man. Slowly she moved forward until she was perhaps fifty yards down the narrow strip of white sand from where he sat. She might have to wait for a while. But it would be better if he turned and saw her, she reasoned.

After spreading out the towel she'd brought, she sat down to wait. But the sun was hot, and after a moment she took off her terry wrap. Shading her eyes, she glanced up quickly at the bright yellow sun. It was brilliant in its own right. But it was also creating a glare on the sand and water. If she sat out here long without protection, even her dark skin would suffer.

Opening her bottle of suntan lotion, she began to smooth it on the silky surface of her arms, legs, and stomach. All the time her eyes were on Craig, willing him to turn around and notice her.

As if her mind had transmitted the message, he finally did raise his head and look in her direction. For a moment he focused directly on her. She even saw his eyebrows lift slightly and the corners of his lips turn up in a male smile of appreciation as he took in the scandalous brevity of her scarlet beach costume.

Laurie was about to raise her hand and wave when he stood up, dusted the sand casually off his long brown legs, and began to stroll in her direction. As he came closer, she felt her heart leap into her throat and searched her mind frantically for something to say. Would "Do you like my new bathing suit?" make a good opening line? she wondered, feeing her cheeks color slightly at the inanity of the thought.

175

To her astonishment Craig didn't pause. Without even giving her a second look, he walked right past and headed toward his house. Laurie's jaw dropped. She hadn't known what to expect from the man. But it certainly wasn't this. Didn't he even care enough about her anymore to be polite?

Her hand went up to touch her face and hit the oversize sunglasses that masked it. Above them the wide brim of her floppy straw hat cast a shadow over her face. Could it be that Craig had seen only her bikini-clad body, not her features, and had therefore not recognized her? After all, he wasn't expecting her. And the Laurie DiMaria he knew would certainly never wear an outfit as daring as this.

The realization floored her. Although the almost naked woman on the beach had definitely caught his attention, he hadn't looked at her very long. She had never known Craig to ignore feminine pulchritude. Yet in this suit hers was certainly on generous display. Could that mean he was so preoccupied by what was on his mind that he wasn't going to even take advantage of the opportunity to ogle an appetizing woman presenting herself to him on a platter? If so, there must be something very important on his mind.

Glancing in the direction of his house, she saw him open the door and disappear inside. For a moment she stared at the barrier. Then, getting up, she put her beach jacket back on and began to march in the direction of the house, determined to find out what, exactly, was on Craig's mind. But when she reached his door and raised her hand to knock, Laurie paused, wondering what she would say when he answered. Unbidden, the question "Didn't you like the way my breasts look in this bathing suit?" popped into her mind. Once more she almost giggled at the wayward direction of her thoughts.

Just then the problem of initiating a conversation was taken out of her hands when Craig threw open the door.

She took in his face quickly, noting the dark circles under his eyes, the days' growth of beard on his cheeks.

"Look here," he said, "this is private property. What are you doing following . . ." And then his voice trailed off as Laurie removed her sunglasses.

"Craig, you know, not recognizing me is getting to be a habit with you."

For a moment he looked stunned, and then another emotion she hoped was pleasure flitted across his face. "Laurie, this is miles from Ann Arbor. What are you doing all the way up here?" he finally asked.

"Isn't it obvious? I came to see you. Well, are you going to let me come in?"

He hesitated for a moment. "I wasn't planning on company," he finally murmured, standing aside.

When she entered the kitchen, she could see how true that last statement was. The counters were littered with half-drunk cups of coffee and uneaten fast food dinners. It was such a complete contrast with Craig's sparkling gourmet kitchen at home that Laurie turned around and stared at him in disbelief.

He shrugged. "I've had a lot on my mind, and it had nothing to do with eating."

This was the opening she'd been hoping for, and before she lost her nerve, she plunged ahead. "So have I," she whispered. "Craig, I need to talk to you."

His expression was wary. "Just why exactly did you come up here? And in that outfit you've got on under your cover-up! That's why I didn't recognize you. I could never picture you wearing a come-on like that."

Laurie gulped. "I know. I bought it this morning and put it on for you."

For a moment they stood looking at each other silently. Then Craig reached out to lay a finger softly on her cheek. "Why for me?"

Laurie turned away, searching for words to explain herself. She didn't find them immediately, and after another moment of silence, Craig took her hand and led her out of the kitchen and into the living room.

"Maybe it'll be easier to talk if there's not a lot of half-eaten food staring at us," he commented dryly.

Laurie couldn't help giggling. His remark had helped to break the tension. The room they were now in was comfortable and old-fashioned. Though Craig hadn't done much to keep this part of the house neat either, it would be an easier place to have a conversation.

Sitting down on the overstuffed sofa, Laurie looked up into Craig's green eyes. His gaze never left her face as he took the seat beside her.

"Laurie," he said, "just now I asked you a question. You didn't answer, but maybe it'll be easier after I tell you what's on my mind." He sighed and leaned back. "This place is such an unholy mess because I haven't been able to think of anything but you since I left Ann Arbor last week. God, I felt like cutting my tongue out after that argument we had. I didn't mean to insult you the way I did. I was just so frustrated and angry. Words spilled out that had no business being said."

Laurie nodded. "I know. It's not all your fault. I said some things I didn't mean either, and I've been regretting them. Craig, you were right about what you said at the arboretum. I *was* confused."

"Confused about what?" He leaned forward, searching her face.

"Mostly about myself, I guess." Her voice was small. "It's been that way for the last year. You don't know what it's like to change your body image so drastically that you don't even recognize the person staring back in the mirror. It's affected my thinking in a lot of peculiar ways."

Craig nodded. "I know. It was like that for me when I changed from an adolescent to a man. Sometimes I used to look in the mirror and expect to see the scrawny kid I used to be."

"But for me it's not just that." Laurie forced herself to continue. "There's more to it. I really haven't had much experience with men, you know, and it was hard for me to see our relationship objectively."

Craig reached out and took her hand. "Laurie, I know how difficult it is for you to admit these things to yourself, let alone say them to me. But I think I do understand. The teen-age Craig Lawson didn't have much experience with girls either. You don't know how much of a relief it was when things changed. After I had matured, women started going after *me*. And not just ordinary women—gorgeous ones."

He sighed. "I've never thought about it before. But I can see now why looks in a female companion became so important to me. The women I dated were just a reassurance that I had escaped my adolescence."

Craig paused and looked away. "But in a sense, I never did. That's really what was wrong with my marriage. I thought I loved my wife, and I was bitter after we broke up. But it wasn't her fault that what we had together was so superficial it couldn't endure. It was really mine."

"Why are you telling me all this?" Laurie broke in.

179

"Because I want to put all my cards on the table. Since that night I ambushed you and Golden Boy, I've been doing some hard thinking about myself, and I haven't liked what I've uncovered." He put his hands together and looked down at his fingertips. "Until I met you, I really didn't know what I wanted from a woman. Actually, until you came along, the relationships I had weren't much better than an adolescent boy's macho fantasies." He gave her a direct look as though afraid of what he might see in her dark eyes. But they held only warm encouragement.

"You know," he went on, "I think my goal was to be self-sufficient, so I really wouldn't have to depend on a woman for anything except sex. That's why I'm a gourmet cook, why I went to such lengths to fix up my house. I think I was really preparing for my lonely old age."

Laurie reached out to touch his hand tenderly. "You said it was hard for me to admit my uncertainties just now. But you're doing the same thing, and it can't be any easier."

He nodded. "I want the air cleared between us, so we can start fresh," he declared.

"Yes," she said. "You seem to be blaming yourself for what happened. But don't forget the most damning piece of evidence against *me*. I accused you of being attracted to my looks, but when I thought about it, I realized that's precisely what first attracted me to *you*. Appreciating your mind and sense of humor followed, but it was the way your facial features fitted together so attractively, the way the muscles in your shoulders rippled under your suit jackets, the way your slacks hugged your narrow hips that first caught my eye."

He opened his mouth to speak, but she shook her head. "There's one thing more I want to say. I wore this skimpy red suit today for a purpose. I wanted to make a statement

180

about something. I've finally come to terms with the old Laurie. She's gone, and she's never coming back." As she spoke, she began to unbelt her terry robe. "This is me now," she said, slipping it off her shoulders and standing up, "and I've accepted the fact."

The old Laurie would have been embarrassed by the expression on Craig's face as his eyes silently took inventory of the woman she had transformed herself into through hard work and perseverance. Slowly, with infinite enjoyment, his warm emerald gaze traveled over her body. He started with her face, lingering on the dark hair that brushed her silky shoulders. Then his eyes moved lower, to her breasts clearly revealed through the scraps of satiny scarlet that only emphasized their shape. Under his scorching inspection, she felt the rounded globes swell and tauten so that the nipples were vividly outlined.

They seemed to be pleading for his attention, yet he didn't move. Cruelly the caress of his gaze abandoned them and slid over the velvety plane of her almond skin and down to the spot between her thighs where the third blazing triangle of silk accented her femininity.

Once more her body responded to his frank scrutiny. His gaze seemed to generate liquid heat under the scarlet cloth, and a burning need began to spread through the core of her body.

"Craig, please," she moaned, not even aware that she had spoken aloud until he sprang from the sofa and pulled her tightly against his long, hard length.

"I can't stand it anymore either," he rasped. "God, Laurie, I love you so much."

She pulled away slightly, but only so that her dark gaze could lock with the intensity of his emerald one. "Do you mean that, Craig?"

"Of course, I mean it. That's one of the things I realized before I came up here, but I think it's been true for a long time, and I just haven't admitted it to myself."

Laurie buried her face in his shoulder. "I didn't know it either for a long time, but I've been in love with you since before I left for Japan. That's one of the reasons I was running away, to escape my feelings for you—feelings I thought you could never possibly return."

Craig's grasp tightened. "Oh, Laurie, never run away from me again. You're everything I've been missing all my life. I need you too much," he declared, tipping her face up so that his lips could mold themselves to hers.

It was a kiss that spoke of longing, need, commitment—a mutual affirmation of their love. It said everything more that needed to be said between the two of them. Before, there had been doubts. Now there was only certainty.

When Craig's lips finally lifted from Laurie's, the two of them were breathless. Laurie clung to him as he rained ardent little kisses over her cheeks, her nose, her neck. When he got to her shoulder, she heard him chuckle deep in his chest.

"What is it?" she asked.

"You taste like coconut," he proclaimed, confirming his words by sliding his tongue over the satiny skin of her shoulder.

"My suntan lotion," Laurie informed him.

Craig grinned. "I thought so. I have the feeling that if I try to make love to you now, you may slip right out of my arms."

Laurie flushed. "I'm sorry. I didn't think . . ." she said.

But he shook his head. "You don't have to apologize. You can take a quick shower. In fact, I'll be glad to wash that lotion off if you like."

182

Laurie pretended to consider the offer, remembering the very sexy shower she and Craig had taken that morning after they had first made love. Then she hadn't known what to expect from their relationship. Now she was no longer troubled by doubts.

Instead of speaking, she simply reached around to her back and undid the scarlet top of her bikini. The scrap of fabric fluttered to the floor.

"Well, that's a pretty direct answer," Craig said approvingly, accepting her invitation and reaching out to caress the sweet mounds of her breasts.

Laurie couldn't suppress a little gasp of pleasure as his thumbs stroked across her nipples.

"I've got to remember that we're heading for the shower first," Craig muttered thickly, taking her hand and leading her toward the bathroom. Once inside the door he turned to adjust the water while Laurie slipped out of the rest of her beach costume.

"I can't get out of my clothes quite that fast," he complained, his eyes lingering on her curves as he began to unbutton his shirt. "And since I haven't shaved today, or yesterday either," he added ruefully, "why don't you start your shower while I do that?"

Smiling seductively, she stepped under the hot spray and slowly pulled the curtain back into place. As she reached for the bar of soap in the dish on the wall, her whole body felt alive with anticipation. Apparently Craig was feeling the same, for it seemed she had barely lathered her arms and legs and rinsed them off, when a taut male form joined her under the steamy water. For a moment he stood behind her, cupping her breasts and seeming to savor their wet, smooth texture against his palms. When they began to swell, the nipples tautening with desire, he moved closer, brushing the back of her body with the front of his.

She leaned her head back against his shoulder and pressed against him. One of his hands moved downward, stroking her flat stomach and then the curve of her hip before finding its way to her thighs.

"You feel very clean," he murmured in her ear before nibbling delicately on the lobe. Playfully he licked her shoulder. "And the coconut is gone. Now all I taste is your delicious skin."

While his lips continued to tease her shoulder, his fingers twined themselves in the downy softness between her legs so that the tremors of excitement that had been coursing through her body seemed to find a home in the sensitive spot his hand was now exploring so knowingly.

When she felt she would melt with the languorous tumult he was creating in her lower body, he suddenly turned her toward him. Abruptly Craig pulled her against the length of his hard form and wrapped his sinewy arms around her.

"I don't know if I can stand still for this shower," he growled. "Do you have any idea what I've been going through this past week—thinking about you, wanting you?"

Sensually he pressed his lean length closer to hers, and she felt the truth of what he said. He was very aroused, and his excitement fueled her own. Shivers of anticipation coursed through her, weakening her legs so that she wasn't sure they could support her weight much longer. She sagged against him, molding her body to his.

"Oh, Craig," she moaned, raising her face for his kiss. As the warm water streamed over their entwined naked bodies, his lips descended on hers, hot and insistent. Her mouth opened willingly before his onslaught so that his tongue, in an imitation of the act of love, could plumb the secrets of

184

the warm cavity. But as he moved inside her mouth, she did not remain passive. Eagerly her tongue met and twined with his, signaling her readiness for yet a further intimacy.

In the next moment Craig's mouth pulled away from hers. Effortlessly he lifted her off her feet and arched her back so that his lips would have free access to her breasts. She closed her eyes and sighed with pleasure as she felt him drop soft kisses on them and then, after circling the nipples with his tongue, suck gently on their pulsing tips.

Currents of heat seemed to ray out from her breasts, streaming through her body so that her bones felt liquefied. When he let her slide sensuously down the length of his aroused flesh and set her back down on her feet, she was unable to support her weight and threw her arms around his neck.

"Oh, God, Craig, make love to me," she whispered urgently in his ear.

One of his arms was around her waist, supporting her, while his other hand had gone once more to the aching area between her thighs.

"Do you want to dry off and use my bed?" he whispered in her ear before dropping a line of stinging kisses along her jaw.

When she was able to think clearly enough to speak, Laurie shook her head and whispered back, "No. I want you to make love to me right here."

"Like this, in the shower?"

"Yes."

"Good, because that's what I want, too," he said huskily, leaning her against the wall so that her weight was braced against it with her legs wide enough apart to admit his eager embrace.

Kissing her breasts once more and burying his face for a

moment in their flushed softness, he flexed his knees and joined his hips to hers. In the next ecstatic moment she felt the thrust of his masculinity. He entered her deeply, filling the aching need he had made within her and creating a new ache.

For a moment he didn't move but merely stood pressed against her, their bodies locked while the water streamed down and pounded a rhythmic tattoo against the tile walls. Her ears were filled with the sound, deafening her to everything but the rush of her blood and the pounding of Craig's heart against her breast.

Almost as soon as he began to move inside her, she felt the tiny world they had created for themselves explode with indescribable sensations. And she knew it was the same for him as he arched his back and gasped with pleasure at his release.

For a few moments more they stood clinging together under the warm, pelting water, savoring the beauty of their tumultuous reunion.

"I love you so much, Laurie," he whispered in her ear.

"I love you, too," she whispered back. "I've always loved you."

He stroked her hair and then chuckled. "I hate to break this up. But this old place only has a thirty-five-gallon water tank. If we stay here much longer, this lovely warm dream we're having is going to turn into a cold shower."

Laurie giggled. "We can't have that."

After turning off the water, Craig reached for a towel. But instead of drying himself, he began to rub her hair and shoulders.

"God, it feels so good to have you here like this. I called this a dream, but it isn't, is it, Laurie? This is going to last for the rest of our lives, isn't it?"

Laurie's dark gaze searched his green one. "It will as far as I'm concerned."

"And you'll never walk out on me again?" he said insistently, searching her features intently. "I don't think I could take that."

"I know I couldn't either," she answered.

The corners of Craig's mouth quirked. "Then can I consider this our engagement shower?"

"Craig!" she sputtered. But even as she protested, she couldn't repress her own grin.

"Is it a bargain? Will you marry me?" he asked persistently.

After flinging her arms around his lean waist, Laurie buried her face against his chest. "You know, when I was a little girl, I used to wonder what it would be like when Mr. Right came along and proposed. But I never pictured it like this."

"You're not answering the question," he growled.

"Oh, Craig, of course I'll marry you."

She hadn't realized how tensely he'd been waiting. But as soon as she said the words, his whole body relaxed, and he beamed down at her before joyfully scooping her up in his arms.

"Well, now that that's all settled, how in the world will we spend the next week?" he demanded wickedly.

From under her coal black lashes, Laurie gave him a coy look. "I can't imagine. Do you have any board games to occupy our time?"

Craig shook his head. "No, but I can guarantee you won't be bored," he said as he carried her to the bed.

It was several hours later before they got around to continuing the conversation they'd begun when Laurie had first arrived.

"I know it seems crazy now, but I was terrified that you'd turn me away when I arrived at your door," Laurie admitted. "In fact, I had a nightmare about it."

Craig wrapped his arm around her naked shoulder and drew her close under the sheet. "This whole week has been a nightmare for me, Laurie. In fact, last night I was cursing myself for a fool because I'd let you get away."

"Is that what you were so angry about?" she asked.

"What are you talking about?"

Laurie grinned weakly. "Well, I guess I have another confession to make. I arrived in town yesterday afternoon. And last night I got up the courage to drive out here. It was already dark, and I could see you through the living-room window. You looked so angry that I turned tail and ran. In fact, I almost gave the whole thing up then and went back to Ann Arbor."

"Oh, Laurie, I'm damn glad you didn't," Craig murmured, pulling her even closer. "You know, when I was looking out into the darkness, I was picturing your face and thinking about how I'd lost you."

"And I had the feeling that you were looking at me," Laurie added.

He dropped a kiss on her forehead and smiled warmly into her eyes. "Listen, Laurie, you and I are going to make each other a promise. We're never going to sit around and guess what the other one is thinking. From now on, if we have problems, we're going to talk about them."

"Yes," she said. "You're right. I'm never going to make stupid assumptions where our relationship is concerned. It's too important."

Craig nodded. "Okay, now that we have the groundwork laid, I have an important question to ask."

"Yes?"

"I'm getting hungry, but the kitchen is a mess. I realize that's entirely my fault, but do I have to clean it up myself—or will you help me?"

Laurie looked at his mock pleading expression and grinned. "Any mess of yours is a mess of mine, partner," she said, throwing off the sheet and reaching for his bathrobe.

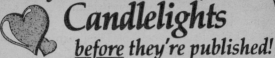

All-new

Candlelight Newsletter

An exceptional, *free* offer awaits readers of Dell's incomparable Candlelight Ecstasy and Supreme Romances.

Subscribe to our all-new CANDLELIGHT NEWSLETTER and you will receive—at absolutely no cost to you—exciting, exclusive information about today's finest romance novels and novelists. You'll be part of a select group to receive sneak previews of upcoming Candlelight Romances, well in advance of publication.

You'll also go behind the scenes to "meet" our Ecstasy and Supreme authors, learning firsthand where they get their ideas and how they made it to the top. News of author appearances and events will be detailed, as well. And contributions from the Candlelight editor will give you the inside scoop on how she makes her decisions about what to publish—and how *you* can try your hand at writing an Ecstasy or Supreme.

You'll find all this and more in Dell's CANDLELIGHT NEWSLETTER. And best of all, *it costs you nothing.* That's right! It's Dell's way of thanking our loyal Candlelight readers and of adding another dimension to your reading enjoyment.

Just fill out the coupon below, return it to us, and look forward to receiving the first of many CANDLELIGHT NEWSLETTERS—overflowing with the kind of excitement that only enhances our romances!

Candlelight
Ecstasy Romances™

$1.95 each

At your local bookstore or use this handy coupon for ordering:

DELL BOOKS—Dept B579C
P.O. BOX 1000, PINE BROOK, N.J. 07058-1000

Please send me the books I have checked above. I am enclosing $ _____ (please add 75c per copy to cover postage and handling). Send check or money order—no cash or C.O.D.'s. Please allow up to 8 weeks for shipment.

Name _____

Address _____

City _____ State Zip _____